A. L. TIPPETT

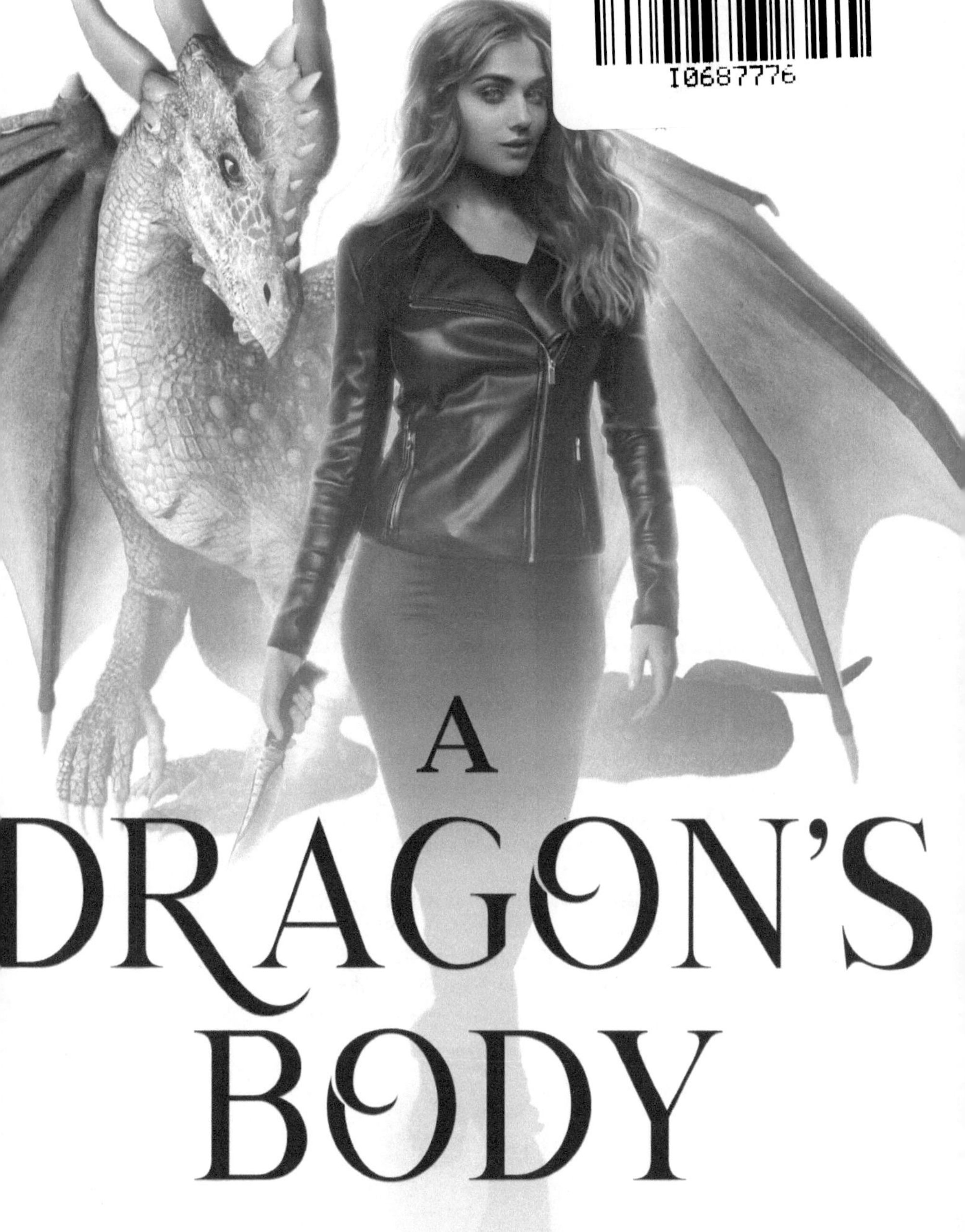

A DRAGON'S BODY

THE MINATH CHRONICLES

BOOK 2

Ebook ISBN: 978-0-6488121-2-8
Paperback ISBN: 978-0-6488121-6-6
Cover designed by MiblArt
Published by Fire Fly Books

British spelling and grammar used throughout this book

STOP!

If you don't enjoy the sweet torture of a cliffhanger ending, then don't read any further! Unless, of course, you
are in possession of the final instalment, *A Dragon's Soul*.

If that's the case, then go right ahead.

CONTENTS

PROLOGUE
~TWO YEARS AGO~

"Hush, students. Some respect for the judge, please," murmured Professor Tormund, a greying hippogryph and also their history teacher.

Sera entered the Mandar City Courthouse once more, along with the nineteen other apprentices in her class. Each year the Mandar Institute for Negotiators, Alchemists, Trackers and Hunters, better known as MINATH, inducted five pupils for each profession for a four-year apprenticeship. Sera had just celebrated her twentieth birthday and entered her final year.

"Hush," the hippogryph repeated sternly, glaring from beneath his feathery eyebrows at the Hunter apprentices in particular. Tormund was the only mythic on the teaching staff at MINATH, but the best one there, in Sera's opinion. He had brought the entire class out today to watch the sentencing of a court case because, in his words, "Today's sentence could be tomorrow's history lesson. We are here to observe the end result of your job. Never forget, every mythic you bring in is an individual with their own life. They have dreams and fears and family, just like you. Make sure you don't bring in the wrong one."

The whispering and sniggering quietened as the judge took her place at the bench. Sera's friend Hazel, an Alchemist-in-training, nudged her and jerked her head behind them. Sera followed her gaze to see two grey-uniformed guards from the Iniques Rehabilitation Centre wheel in a frame that held a sealed glass cube. A collective gasp escaped the students as they saw the mythic trapped inside the tempered glass. It was a shadow. The unique mythic was rarely seen and tended to live on the fringes of society. The black smoke that obscured its true form pulsed slowly as the guards set the cell to the right of Judge Lenka. Glancing at the internal door past the judge's bench, Sera watched as the jury filed into the courtroom. Running her eyes over the group, she analysed them with a frown.

Something seems... off.

She flinched as she sensed Professor Tormund leaning over her shoulder. He whispered into her ear so softly that she had to strain to hear his words over the clicking of his beak.

"I see your scrutiny. Have you noticed that all the jury members are humans?"

Returning her gaze to the jury, she realised he was right. There were ten humans shuffling to their seats, the majority of whom were men.

Mimicking his volume, she whispered, "Somehow it doesn't seem fair for it to be only humans that pass judgement on a mythic. Like... it's 'them' against 'us.' Like we're better than them."

Keeping her focus forward, she saw him nod in her peripheral, satisfied with her evaluation. His expression dropped and he muttered darkly, "This won't be a fair sentence." Before Sera could ask what he meant, he straightened, his feathered head too high for her to subtly request an explanation.

The judge cracked her gavel as the jury took their seats. The shadow throbbed in time with the sharp sound. Tendrils of the mist warped and began to vibrate slightly as the judge cleared her throat.

"Thank you all for your time today. I ask the jury, have you made a decision?"

"Yes, we have, your Honour."

"The shadow, Inca Soleque, stands accused of murder in the first degree of Hector Dower. How does the jury find?"

"We find Inca Soleque guilty."

A wail echoed from the cell as Inca's vibrations grew in strength and they pounded against the glass.

"I didn't do it," they screeched, their voice warping between high and low notes. "You know it! I am innocent."

Judge Lenka spoke over the shadow, projecting her voice so the crowd would hear the sentence. "I hearby sentence the shadow, Inca Soleque, to death by electrocution."

"No," they howled, the black tentacles solidifying and smacking their prison as the shadows spiralled and swirled, growing and filling the space as they vented their fear and rage. "You can't do this," Inca sobbed.

Sera turned away, her heart twisting with compassion. She sternly reminded herself that the shadow had murdered an old man in his own home, and she shouldn't feel sympathy for the killer. Hardening her expression, Sera raised her eyes back to the shadow and, just for a moment, red eyes stared out at her before the darkness closed around their form once more.

The Hunters jeered at the shadow as the glass cage was wheeled from the courtroom before Professor Tormund swung a wing out and clipped the closest one, Tyler, around his ears. Tyler rubbed the side of his head and shot a venomous look towards his teacher. Sera turned away in disgust at Tyler's attitude. He might be the best

Hunter in their year, but he was an arrogant jerk. She had no time for him. The hippogryph's mouth pulled down in grief as the screams of the shadow faded once the door closed behind them.

Sera placed a hand on his grey coat and said, "I didn't enjoy that either, but at least Hector Dower has justice now."

Her teacher regarded her for a long moment before turning away. He muttered, "Does he, though?"

CHAPTER ONE

~ARIUS~

ARIUS ROARED HIS PAIN and frustration to the dawning sun. Five nights had passed since the storm knocked him unconscious and speared him and Seraphina into Lake Eyre, but the brightening sky did nothing to ease his agony. When he had awoken at sunset in the shallows of the lake, it had taken him a moment to realise his Soulbound was missing as the debilitating pain of his broken wing overwhelmed all other thoughts. Once he'd realised Sera was gone, he'd been swept into a frenzy. He'd splashed clumsily along the shoreline, dragging his useless wing, and desperately scanned the murky depths of the water, praying to the Four Gods she hadn't been killed in the crash. Once his inner turmoil subsided enough for rationality to return, Arius realised he could still sense her soul. The relief of knowing she was alive was swiftly overtaken by fear for her safety.

The past five days had been long, painful and full of worry. A void enveloped his chest, deepening his fear. He was afraid that she'd come to harm after the fall. He was angry that he couldn't help her in his current state. What was the use of all his magic if he was useless to save the one he loved? Arius slammed his tail into the closest tree, the trunk snapping as if it were no more than a twig. His fury and fear constricted his throat, blinding him from logical thought. To release his pain, he spewed forth a pillar of flame and set the forest alight. Panting, he glared at the flames licking the foliage. After a minute of watching the trees burn, he sighed. He shouldn't take his anger out on Ghaia's creations. Before the blaze could take hold he quelled the magic of his flames and the would-be forest fire died. Once the fire had completely vanished, he dropped his head to the shaly shore of the lake and sank to his belly. Melancholy gripped him and he howled his fears to Caelhi, the Goddess of the Air. She cared for all creatures belonging to the sky, so surely she would hear his pleas to look after his Soulbound, even though Sera was one of Ghaia's children.

The pain was destroying him. Not from his wing; that would be fully healed in a few more days. A jagged hole had torn through his chest ever since he'd sensed Sera travelling further away from him. Now her soul was only a dim speck in the horizon of his consciousness. He had a vague sense that she was east of him, so assumed she had returned to Mandar City. Doubt slipped into his mind, warping his reason, and he wondered if she wasn't hurt. Perhaps she'd decided to leave him. He didn't understand how she could have abandoned him so casually. While Arius understood that she had led a life before him and had a family back in the city, he thought she wouldn't have been able to resist the will of the Gods. They were Soulbound. But even before the binding, he thought he had meant something to her. Why would she leave him? He whined low in his throat. As soon as he was fully healed he would fly to confront her, but in the meantime he just had to keep stumbling his way toward the city.

He rose grimly to his feet once more and marched on, dragging his broken wing. Even though it exposed him to prying eyes, he'd purposely kept his journey beside Lake Eyre since it was easier for a mythic of his size to travel in the open, especially when injured. The last thing he wanted was for his wing to get snagged on trees and bushes the entire time he was travelling.

Something small unexpectedly buzzed past his right ear and he shook his head in annoyance. The whirring sounded again in his other ear followed by a high-pitched snigger. Nostrils flaring, he realised it was one of those damnable titters. The annoying little birds would whisper derisively between themselves and tease all who crossed their path, although it was rare to see them this far from civilisation. Another mocking snicker sounded from behind him. He swung his head and snapped his fangs at the nearest titter. Inspiration struck as his jaws closed on empty air and he stopped his hostile behaviour and sat back on his haunches.

"Titter, show yourself. I, Arius, son of Talegar and Valenta, wish to speak to you."

Two titters appeared in front of him before landing on his snout. He growled low at their impertinence. The birds giggled nervously and fluttered to a nearby branch.

"Hiya, big lizard. Hiya! What wrong with your wing?" the male of the pair called out.

The female pecked her mate and whispered, "Hush! Great dragon eat you if you rude, eat you!"

"He not eat me, I too quick for him while he only got one wing."

"What about when he better?" The second titter cuffed the male over the head with her white wing. He squawked indignantly but snapped his black beak shut.

Arius waited patiently for their squabbling to end. "I have a task for you. Your help will earn my deep gratitude. I need you to take a message to someone for me."

The titters eyed him suspiciously and whispered to one another. The female titter eventually puffed her blue breast up with pride and said, "This great honour, mighty dragon."

The male interjected, "Where message going?"

"I believe she's in Mandar City. I'm not sure precisely where. Her name is Seraphina but you may hear her called Sera. She's a young woman with beautiful auburn hair, tanned skin and a smattering of freckles across her cheeks. She has a golden scar on her palm. She carries a knife named Firinne in a sheath on her belt. She is a Tracker for the MRO so will likely be wearing her green uniform."

They had been nodding along, absorbing his description, but screeched at that. "A Tracker! We no help them!"

"She's different to other Trackers. She has bound herself to me and will help us in the future."

They muttered sullenly under their breath, feathers fluffed in protest. A rumble built in his throat at their reluctance and his chest glowed with barely contained fire. He bared his fangs at the titters, so trapped in his own fear of losing his Soulbound that he refused to acknowledge theirs.

"Fine, fine," acquiesced the female. "We do what you ask. What we say to her?"

The flames that had begun licking his throat subsided and he forced himself to relax. He let the breath he'd been holding out in a rush and murmured, "Thank you." He bowed his head. "I need you to find her and tell her Arius is on his way. If she's hurt or imprisoned, tell her I'm coming to save her. I need her to be safe. I need her with me." He bit back the emotion that threatened to overwhelm him again and ducked his head momentarily. Raising his emerald eyes to look into the red eyes of the titters, he said, "I will owe you a favour if you do this for me. Once you have delivered the message, find me." With a grimace, he flexed his injured wing and said, "By that time, I will have returned to the skies. Fly fast, little ones, and find my love."

CHAPTER TWO

SERA STARED BLANKLY AT her computer. The words swam on the screen as she struggled to focus on the report she was typing up. It had been five days since she had been found on the road into Mandar City with no memory of what happened to her. She had been relegated to desk duties until she received clearance from the Mythic Relations Office's medical team. The fact that she couldn't remember anything from the eleven days she'd been gone didn't help her case. So, for the time being, she was stuck in the office transcribing hard copies of reports from forty years ago onto the MRO's online filing system.

The morning sunlight streamed through the windows that lined one side of the Tracker's Hub, practically begging her to leave the stuffy office and take Balthazar out for a training ride. She tapped her fingers aimlessly against the arm of her office chair and leaned back. It creaked and rolled away from the desk. She huffed in frustration and tugged herself closer to the screen. The pile of paperwork to her right teetered precariously. She glared at it. Shoving her chair away, she stood up with the intention of straightening the pile but the wheels caught on a loose strand in the carpet and stalled its movement. Growling under her breath, she leant down to unwind the snag from the wheel.

"Tracker Seraphina?"

She twisted and rose hastily to see who had summoned her but cracked her head on the underside of her desk. "For Ghaia's sake!" She rubbed the spot as she staggered upright, eyes watering.

Negotiator Aaron stood in front of her desk wearing a bemused smile. "Sorry to bother you, but I wanted to see how you were going with the archives?"

She glanced at the tower of reports that still threatened to collapse, raised an eyebrow at him and asked blandly, "How does it look like I'm going?"

He chuckled nervously, running a dark-skinned hand over his cropped black hair. "It does look like a big job, but I'm sure you will get it completed in no time." He offered her an encouraging grin as he walked around her desk and helped to straighten the reports.

She dropped her shoulders and sighed. *It's not his fault that I'm stuck here.* She returned his smile and said, "Thanks, Negotiator Aaron. I appreciate the help. Sorry I've been short with you."

He beamed at her and said, "Just call me Aaron." He waved a hand dismissively and continued, "No need to apologise. I am just so thrilled that someone is finally moving the records across. Once we have easy access to all that precious information, we will be able to analyse the data to see whether there are any correlations between the activities of the mythics from then to now. Just imagine if we could use forty years of data to predict potential threats before they happen and could actually help those mythics before they start down the wrong path. The opportunities are endless!"

His enthusiasm was infectious and, even though she hated the job, Sera felt a renewed sense of motivation to complete her task, now that there was a purpose. She nodded to him and sat back down. "I'd better get back onto it, then."

He flashed her a winning smile and ran his hands over his head again. "Before I go... I was just wondering whether you were going with anyone to the ceremony this weekend?"

She stared at him blankly and asked, "What ceremony?"

"The Choosing Ceremony for this year's graduates from MINATH."

"Oh! I'd forgotten about that."

"All previous graduates were invited; didn't you get a letter?" Aaron quirked an eyebrow.

"Yeah, I did. Sorry, I forgot." She scrubbed a hand over her face before explaining, "My housemate, Hazel – she's an Alchemist here – she's on the organising committee. It's all she's been talking about lately. I've just... had a lot on my mind." She lifted her lips at the Negotiator in a tired approximation of a smile.

He placed a comforting hand on her shoulder and Sera froze at his touch.

Relax. He's not Tyler. He's not going to hurt you.

Unaware of her discomfort, Aaron said, "I can only imagine." He smiled sympathetically. "I heard what happened. It must be so frustrating having lost some of your memories. If there's anything I can do to help, please tell me." He ducked his head bashfully as he added quickly, "I'd be more than happy to accompany you if you would like?"

Before Sera could respond, he walked away with his eyes on the floor, a dark hue staining his cheeks.

Three hours later a headache pounded through her skull. She rubbed her eyes and pinched the bridge of her nose. With a couple of clicks, she finalised the last few details and saved the report.

Ten down, only two hundred to go.

Reaching forward, she placed her thumb against the corner of her monitor and, with a flash of blue light that scanned her fingerprint, it automatically signed her out and turned the screen off. She sighed and rolled her chair away from her desk. Standing up, she stretched briefly, her back cracking from having been in the one position for so long. Grabbing her phone, she exited her cubicle, nearly running into Hazel.

"Hey, Sera!" her friend and housemate said warmly. With a quick assessment, she smiled sympathetically and asked, "Rough day?"

"Ridiculous," Sera groaned. "Getting there slowly, but I need a break."

Concern flashed over Hazel's face but she hid it swiftly behind a cheerful smile. "I was coming to see if you wanted to join me for lunch? I was going to head over to Tregua Park. After the morning I've had, I need some fresh air. I figured you could use some too." Hazel held up two takeaway coffees and offered one to Sera.

Sera lifted her cheeks in what she hoped looked like a smile. "Sounds great." Try as she might, she couldn't summon the energy to sound more than slightly interested.

"Let's go to Donny's. He makes the best chicken wraps."

"Sure, sure. Whatever you want. So long as I don't need to look at a screen, I don't really care what we eat."

Hazel chuckled as she slipped her arm companionably through Sera's. "No problem. Let's go." After a brief silence as they wound their way through the half empty office, Hazel asked, "So, how are you going, Sera? Really?" She raised an eyebrow as she studied her friend.

Shrugging nonchalantly, Sera muttered, "I've still got some bumps and bruises but I'm okay."

"You know that's not what I meant. I will come back to that question, but while we're on the topic, how's that scar on your hand?"

"It's weird." Sera pouted. "The original wound is completely healed but it's scarred up in this weird gold colour. And I don't know how to explain it properly but it tingles underneath the skin. Nothing I do eases it. And the bruise in the crook of my elbow is still painful, too. This will sound dumb," she hesitated and dropped her eyes, "but I feel like my memory loss has something to do with it."

Hazel gently took her hand as they walked and turned it over, rubbing her thumb tenderly over the palm. The elevator doors hissed open and the disembodied voice of the MRO's Artificial Intelligence, Frank, echoed out of the lift. "You have arrived at Level Three, housing the Tracker's Hub."

Sera was so engrossed in studying her hand with Hazel she nearly ran into a Tracker exiting the elevator.

"Watch it!" the woman barked.

"Tracker Helena!" Sera leapt back, nearly crashing into Hazel in the process. "I'm so sorry, ma'am. I wasn't watching where I was going."

The Head Tracker was an ornery woman with grey strands spreading through her black locks and lines etched deep in her face from years in the sun. She was a talented Tracker but now spent most of her days arranging the assignments for the Trackers under her care and giving the occasional training session at MINATH. She glared at the two younger women and grunted.

"Tracker Seraphina. I was just coming up to tell you I received your application to resume field work, but now I wonder whether you are ready. Your head doesn't seem to be in the right space yet."

"Please, ma'am, I have to get back out there. Being stuck behind a desk isn't helping me at all. I know I can do it."

"The medical team haven't figured out what caused your amnesia. Understandably, they are reluctant to put you at risk in case it worsens while you're out on a mission."

"I'm doing the meditation exercises they've given me, and there's been no sign of me losing any more of my memories. Please, I need to do my job. I'm going crazy sitting in front of a screen all day. I'm sure if I felt more like my old self, my memories would eventually come back. Please, Tracker Helena." She was begging now but she didn't care. "I need a purpose. One that doesn't involve transcribing forty-year-old paperwork!"

Tracker Helena sighed. "All right. If it will shut you up, I'll sign off on your request. But get your head on straight, girl. I don't want to regret my decision." Something caught her attention and she paused, then pursed her lips. Snatching Sera's hand, she demanded, "What's this on your palm?"

"You mean my scar? I got it on my trip but I can't remember how."

"Hmmm. That's odd." Releasing her hand abruptly, as if it had burnt her, Tracker Helena scanned Sera's face intently before sighing. "I knew someone else who had one of these. They're long gone now." Grief flitted across her face, quickly replaced by confusion. Noticing Sera's searching look, she rearranged her features into their usual scowl.

"Please, ma'am, can you tell me who had a scar resembling mine? Where did they get theirs from?"

Something akin to fear flashed in her eyes, and the older woman lowered her voice. "This is not the place to discuss such things." Louder, she said, "Meet me at the stables tomorrow afternoon and we'll go for a training session to ensure you're ready to return to field work." Nodding dismissively to the two friends, she turned and strode away.

CHAPTER THREE

DONNY, THE TAURON AT the Mandar City Market, passed them their wraps. Sera eyed him in disdain. He might be a talented baker, but last month she'd seen him treat a young homeless boy like he was a rogue werewolf. After the kid had attempted to steal a pastry Donny had pinned him down with his cloven hoof so hard it looked as if the boy was going to suffocate. She'd offered to pay for the food but the half-man, half-bull wanted to teach the boy a lesson. Luckily, he escaped, but every now and then she caught herself wondering about the child.

No, the kid shouldn't have stolen, but it was obvious he was starving. Where was Donny's compassion?

Clutching their lunch and coffees to their chest, they left the stall and wound their way through the market. Leading the way, Hazel took them to the Sotor River where they sat down on a bench. Ever since she woke up on the road in the dark with no memories from her camping trip, a black cloud had clung to Sera. The gloom had settled into her bones, making it hard to find joy in anything. Anger constantly rippled just below the surface of her emotions, ready to burst out at any inconvenience.

Fuck this shit. I'm so over this.

She itched the inside of her elbow. The bruise was healing, but she had no idea how she got it.

"Okay," Hazel began as she took a sip of coffee, "talk to me. We haven't really had a chance to have a proper chat since you came home. How are you?"

"Honestly? Pretty shit. It's a surreal feeling to know that over a week passed without having any knowledge of the things that happened in that time. I can see the physical marks on my body and feel the ache in my muscles, so I can't have just lain in a coma the entire time. The not-knowing is eating away at me. I just know that something important happened but there is no memory." Tears stung her eyes and she lifted her chin to look out over the river, clenching her jaw in an effort to hold back the emotions that threatened to overwhelm her.

"I'm so sorry I haven't been around much lately. I feel bad that I haven't been there for you. I didn't realise how much you were struggling."

"I realise you've been busy with the committee organising the Choosing. You can't spend your life worrying about mine."

Hazel's eyebrows kissed. "Well, I do." Noticing the shine in Sera's eyes, she wrapped her arms around her friend and whispered, "It's okay to cry."

Buckling into Hazel's embrace, Sera let go. She wept, allowing the strange grief for her lost memories to wash over her. Sobs wracked her body as frustration took over and she balled her fists against Hazel's back. The release of her grief was cathartic. Slowly, her cries eased and she took a few shuddering breaths and pushed away, mustering up a watery smile.

Rubbing her back, Hazel asked, "Do you feel a little better?"

Sera nodded and wiped her tears away on her sleeve. Her friend kept rubbing her back comfortingly and suggested, "How about we talk it through. Tell me everything you remember before and after the blank spot in your memory. Tell me about your injuries and let's see if we can piece together what happened."

"Well, I left the house Saturday morning as planned. I hiked into the mountains and shot a doe." Sera frowned in concentration. "I can recall skinning it, cooking a piece for dinner and putting the rest of the venison in a sack in a tree. Then everything is blank. The more I focus on it, the more it's like," she waved her hand vaguely in the air, "there's a wall in my mind I can't get past."

"That's odd that it cuts off like that." Hazel wore a puzzled expression. "What's your next memory?"

Shrugging, she said, "Waking up in the dark on the dirt road that leads up to Grave's Point. I stumbled towards the city lights until Balthazar found me. He brought me to the MRO where the medics looked after me."

"And what about your injuries? Tell me about all of them, no matter how small."

"You already know about the weird scar on my palm and the bruise in the crook of my elbow. I have a clean cut on my other arm that I think is from a knife. There's another scar across my chest that's healed the same golden colour as my hand. I've got some chafing between my legs. I have no idea what it's actually from but it kind of looks like I've been riding for a long time in a saddle, wearing shorts. I have some weird pricks on my hand and chest, as if something held me down with a claw the size of a hand. They've almost healed now but I have a cut on the inside of my cheek, which still hurts. Other than that, just the usual muscle tightness that comes from a mountain hike."

"Can I look inside your mouth, please?"

Sera nodded and opened her mouth wide, tilting her head so the sunlight would expose the injury.

"Shit, Sera!" Hazel exclaimed when she saw the cut inside her cheek. "That looks infected. Why didn't you say something sooner?"

Sera drew her brows together quizzically. "It hurts a bit, but it doesn't feel that bad. I haven't really looked in the mirror much since coming home, so I didn't realise there was anything wrong."

Hazel stared at her, horrified. "You and I are going home right now so I can fix you up."

"But what about work?"

"Screw work. I'll tell them I had to take you home because you're sick."

Sera opened her mouth to protest but her friend held up a hand, halting her grumble.

"I'm not taking no for an answer. Let's go."

CHAPTER FOUR

EXITING THE LIFT INSIDE their apartment building, the two friends turned right and followed the corridor until they reached Room 113. Swiping the Personal Security Band attached to her wrist against the control panel on the door, Hazel entered first and made a beeline for her work station. Sera followed slowly, but stopped when Perry stalked in front of her and sat down, tail twitching. Perry was Hazel's cat, a tabby she'd rescued last year. The mangy thing adored Hazel but would take any opportunity to attack Sera – and anyone else who came to the apartment, for that matter. Glaring at the tomcat, she circled warily around him and joined Hazel. Her friend handed her a bottle of white liquid.

"This is a prototype I've been working on. It's basically the same as Heal but it's edible. Put it on the inside of your cheek and hopefully it will clear up that nasty sore."

Sera did as she was bid, biting back a wince from the sting as the new version of Heal began its work. To distract herself she watched as Hazel busily pulled down tubs and bottles of various plants, oils and minerals from the timber shelves attached to the wall. Not for the first time, Sera admired Hazel's desk while she waited for her friend to commence her creation process. It was a beautifully rustic thing, made of rosewood with curved corners and a hint of the original tree's bark on the edge. There was a hole on the surface where a defect in the timber had been cut out, creating a perfect slot for her mortar bowl. Hazel carefully arranged each container onto the worn desk and rested her pestle in the mortar.

"What are you creating?" Sera asked.

"I'm going to attempt something no one has ever done before," Hazel said with a wink. "I'm going to try to bring your memory back."

Sera's eyebrows shot up. *If anyone can do something this complex, it's Hazel.*

Before she began, Hazel picked up a piece of fluorite that permanently sat at the back of the desk and touched it to her forehead, then her lips. Closing her eyes, she held it over her heart and stroked the purple and green crystal. Sera watched on with a slight smile. Every time Hazel performed alchemy at home she followed this ritual.

"I see you smiling, Sera. I know you think it's silly, but the fluorite helps me focus. Why do you think I'm so good at alchemy?"

"To be honest, I believe it's because you studied hard at MINATH and practise a lot. What other Alchemist has their own work station at home? But hey, if you feel the crystals help you, who am I to disagree?"

Hazel shot her an exasperated look. "I truly believe they help me to find my inner peace, Sera. Personally, I think you should give them more credit and try using crystals yourself. You might be surprised."

"Fair enough." Sera raised her hands in defeat. "Teach me the magic of the crystals, oh wise one."

Her friend snorted and rolled her eyes but explained anyway. "They're not magic, exactly. They just help to channel your own energies. Each crystal has a purpose. Fluorite helps me find clarity and focus. I use my prehnite point at work to help me stay calm. I keep amethyst beside my bed to ward off bad dreams. Before my family moved to Mandar City, they used crystals as part of their daily ritual in Soldenheim."

Sera squinted and asked, "Remind me, Soldenheim is North-East? Across the Kaldern Ocean, yeah?"

Hazel nodded. "That's right." As she spoke, she lit a stick of sage and waited for the flame to take hold before gently blowing it out and coaxing the embers forward. "Not many boats travel there these days, so I've never met most of my cousins. My grandparents immigrated to Mandar when my mother was only six-years-old and they still use their crystals here. When I followed in Mum's footsteps and became an Alchemist, she showed me how to harness their power to enhance my experiments." She smudged the sage around Sera and commanded, "Breathe deep."

Turning back to her desk, Hazel picked up a container and shook some small blue stone chips into her mortar and used her pestle to crush them. She explained as she worked, "This is azurite stone. Azurite is excellent for boosting your memory." She placed a few sprigs of lavender into the bowl and set about grinding again. "The lavender helps ease stress, and now," she grabbed a small bottle of oil, "I'll add two drops of lemon oil to improve recall. Three drops of rosemary oil to stimulate the mind and," she unscrewed the lid of a glass jar, "a couple of dried skyberries for mental clarity."

She paused in her mixing and tapped her chin with a fingernail, lost in thought. With a glance at Sera, she smiled and pulled her necklace over her head. A tiny glass vial filled with clear fluid dangled by a chain from her fingertips and she whispered, "This is melted snow from the peaks of Mount Gambrier in Soldenheim. It's supposed to be formed from the frozen tears of Caelhi, the Goddess of the Air." She uncorked the precious liquid and allowed three drops to drip into the mixture. A feminine sigh rose from the bowl along with a flash of white light. Both women gasped at the unexpected reaction and stared at each other with wide eyes.

Hazel reached out with trembling hands and scraped her creation into an unmarked container. "Look, I'm no expert when it comes to memory loss, Sera, but I truly believe this will help. I hope you don't mind me using you as a test subject," she joked with a shaky laugh.

Sera chuckled and shook her head silently, not trusting her own voice to work. She stood still as Hazel wiped the grainy paste onto the centre of her forehead, temples, lips and throat. Acting on instinct, Sera closed her eyes and inhaled, focusing on the intoxicating mixture of scents. She believed in Hazel's abilities as a talented Alchemist but was unsure if amnesia was something one could recover from. However, that wouldn't stop her from continuing to look for a way to bring her memories back. Something shifted in her psyche and she sensed an emptiness in her mind.

As if something is missing that was there before...

She probed her consciousness, hunting for an explanation, and felt a tugging sensation to the west. She wanted to cry from the sudden feeling of longing that pulled at her heart. The ache in her chest was severe and nearly dropped her to her knees. A sense of warmth rushed over her skin and she yearned for the touch of the soul that called to her.

Seraphina...

Someone called her name. She needed to find him.

Who are you? she cried in her mind.

It is Arius, your Soulbound. Our connection is tenuous. Where are you? Let me help you!

Sera wept from the comforting presence that filled her thoughts, even though she couldn't remember his face. She couldn't stop herself from blurting, *I need you.*

I'm on my way, dearest one. Tell me where to find you.

I'm in Mandar City. She could feel their link being forced closed as something dark rose within her body to fight against it.

I'm coming. The last words from Arius echoed in her head before the bond failed. She dropped to the floor and curled into a ball, weeping.

Hazel rushed to her side and wrapped her arms around her. "Sera! What's wrong? Are you hurt? Did the mixture not work?"

"No, no, it did! Sort of. I don't remember but I..." Sera's brows furrowed together. "I felt a connection with someone. But... it's fading." She pummelled the floorboards with her hands and yelled, "I'm forgetting again. I don't remember what just happened!" She wanted to throw something, preferably something heavy that would make a satisfying sound when it shattered the glass window.

Hazel made soothing noises and held Sera as she let her fury out in the form of tears. Once her anger had abated slightly, Hazel murmured, "I'm so sorry it didn't work."

"It's not your fault that my head is mucked up," muttered Sera darkly. "I'm sorry you wasted your special mountain snow on me."

"It wasn't wasted. It's never wasted on you." Hazel squeezed her in a tight hug before standing. "Come on, go have a shower and freshen up and I'll get dinner sorted."

"I should help you," mumbled Sera, wiping her face.

Holding her hand out, Hazel helped Sera to her feet. "To be honest, you're not looking your best," she joked in an attempt to cheer Sera up. "A nice, warm shower will do you a world of good."

Sera placed her hand on her friend's shoulder, meeting her eyes, and said seriously, "Thank you, Hazel. For trying. You are always there for me, and you've gone above and beyond to help me get my memories back. I don't know what I would do without you. I hope you realise how much I appreciate everything you do."

Hazel blushed. "Yeah, yeah, no need to get all sappy," she blustered. "Now let me go so we can eat!"

CHAPTER FIVE

"COME ON, TRACKER SERAPHINA, we're waiting." Tracker Helena sat astride a young unicorn, its chestnut coat glowing in the afternoon sun. As if to get the point across, the unicorn pawed the ground and snorted emphatically. "That will do, Rella." The old woman laid a comforting hand against the filly's neck.

The strange events following Hazel's attempt at getting Sera's memories back last night were fuzzy. Sera knew she'd connected with someone or something but couldn't remember what she'd learnt. She had been looking forward to this training ride through the monotonous paperwork all day. Balthazar was standing nearby, waiting for her, so she dashed into the tack room to grab his bitless bridle, saddle and saddle cloth and tacked up. Tightening the girth, she swung up easily and settled into the seat. The brown leather squeaked as she slipped her boots into the stirrups.

"Move out," the Head Tracker commanded.

With a squeal, Rella jumped into a swift trot, holding her head high as if to show off her pearlescent horn and the amber stones that circled the base. Balthazar blew out a long-suffering sigh before trotting after them. The buckskin stallion's long stride easily matched Rella's and they established a steady rhythm. Their trot was a floating gait and comfortable to sit to. Both Trackers left their reins loose, allowing the unicorns their head. Covering the ground smoothly, it didn't take long for them to pass the farms surrounding Mandar City. Paddocks filled with cattle or crops flew past them. Instead of turning right towards the Kaldern Ocean, they followed a dirt road that curved to the west, towards the mountains. Tendrils of auburn hair escaped Sera's plait as the wind gusted over them. Tracker Helena remained silent, so Sera followed her lead and kept her mouth shut. Looking over her shoulder, Sera could make out the massive dome of wire fencing that was the Iniques Rehabilitation Centre. She shuddered and turned back to watch where they were going.

Leaving the fenced farms behind, they entered a timber plantation. The pine trees were planted in long lines, the unnatural symmetry putting Sera on edge. However, Balthazar's steadying presence eased her troubled thoughts. She was lucky that Balthazar had chosen her as his rider. He'd been partnered with another man for years until Tracker Emmett passed away on a mission the year before Sera had graduated. It was a rare but very real threat in this job. Not everyone came home. Balthazar had grieved for months after his rider died and every now and then Sera would catch him gazing into the distance with a sad expression. He'd never told her the story of how he lost his rider and Sera respected his wish for privacy. At Tracker Helena's command, they slowed to a walk, riding side by side between the long lines of trunks.

Twisting in the saddle to face Sera, Tracker Helena asked, "Do you have your weapons?"

"No, Tracker Helena. I lost my backpack along with both my rifle and my blade during my time away. I've replaced my pack and my MRO Survival Kit but I haven't received a replacement gun yet since I've been on desk duty."

"You can call me Helena when we're alone. You'll be needing a gun for field work. Here," the older woman said, lobbing a box of bullets to Sera before pulling an unloaded pistol from her holster and tossing it to her too.

The unicorns didn't flinch at the weapon being thrown between them. Sera lurched sideways and Balthazar shifted smoothly beneath her, allowing her to snag the bullet box easily but fumbling slightly on the catch of the gun. She weighed it in her hands and admired the intricate engraving on the walnut grip. Raising the barrel, she lined the sights up and stared into the distance, pleased with the balance of the handgun.

"Thank you, Helena. This is a superb weapon."

"Try not to lose this one."

"I won't. May I ask, where is it from? It doesn't appear to be one of the standard issue pistols from the Weapons Department."

"That's because it's not. It was mine from when I was still doing field work."

"What? You can't give me this! You still need it."

"I'm formally retiring from field work this month. I thought I would take young Rella here out for one last training ride before she chooses her rider this weekend. My focus will now be on the training of the MRO's Trackers and assigning missions. I'll also be running occasional classes at MINATH for the apprentices. I won't be needing this weapon anymore. I'd rather see it used and taken care of than sitting locked in my safe at home."

"This is truly a great gift. Thank you. I'm not sure I deserve it, but I will do my best to use it wisely." Taking the offered holster from Helena, she threaded it onto her belt and tucked the gun inside.

Grey eyes scrutinised her closely before Helena's face broke into a rare smile. "I believe you will."

Rella shook her mane and pranced on the spot, waving her tail at Balthazar coyly. The buckskin stallion snorted derisively and ignored her flirting. Helena rested her hand on the filly's neck again and whispered something in her ear. The unicorn calmed down and relaxed into their walk once more. The plantation abruptly gave way to the wilds. Tangled undergrowth surrounded the trees that grew haphazardly through the thick bushes. Without any guidance from their riders, the unicorns followed a narrow path in single file.

They rode on in silence a while longer before Sera mustered up the courage to ask the question that had been plaguing her since yesterday. "You mentioned that you'd seen a scar similar to mine in the past?" she prompted. She held her hand out to reinforce her question.

Helena sighed and scrubbed a hand over her face. "Yes. But perhaps I shouldn't have mentioned it. It's impossible for it to be the same kind of mark."

"Please, tell me what you know."

This could be my only chance to find out what happened to me.

"Don't get your hopes up," Helena warned Sera. "I was a young woman when the Mythic War ended. I'm not proud to say that during the war I was involved in the killing of mythics that didn't deserve to die. There was one that I will never forget." She closed her eyes for a moment as some strong emotion twisted her features. "The last dragon. I was one of the guards watching his cage as we waited for the final decision on his fate. The last night of his life, he spoke to me. He told me his name was Volkuhn and he was ready to die." She paused and took a deep breath. "He'd lost his mate in the war and didn't want to live without her. He called her his Soulbound and showed me the golden scars on the palm of his talon and over his heart where he had pledged himself to her. It's a unique bonding between dragons that they believe is sanctioned by the Four Gods. I never found out her name. They executed him that night. He didn't even put up a fight. It was over forty years ago, but the memory is burnt into my soul." Helena turned her face away whilst she composed herself.

Sera's heart crumbled, not only because of the terrible story, but because she knew now that Helena's knowledge had nothing to do with her scars. The dragon species had died with Volkuhn. Besides, she was only a human. *Helena was right. It is impossible.* Yet a small bubble of rebellion refused to be burst inside her heart. The golden scar over hand and heart was a strange coincidence.

Helena turned back towards Sera and asked pointedly, "I haven't heard the full story from you. What happened to you on that camping trip?"

"I honestly can't remember anything beyond my first night. I remember shooting a doe and skinning it on the Saturday, setting up camp and going to sleep. Then it's just a blank until two Wednesdays later when I found myself on the road into the city with a heap of injuries I don't remember collecting."

"That *is* strange."

"You're telling me!" Sera let go of the reins to undo and plait her wayward hair once more. "It's so frustrating. I have this niggling feeling in the back of my mind that if I can crack some code in my brain, I could unlock everything. It feels like…" she paused and glanced at the dark-haired woman before ploughing on, "like something important happened. Like there was a secret that I learnt, that I've been forced to forget."

Helena examined her with a cocked head before asking, "Have you ever heard of the Little Birds?"

As Sera opened her mouth to deny any knowledge, Rella squealed and shied sideways, crashing into a bush. Helena grabbed a handful of her mane to stay mounted and murmured soothing words, trying to calm the filly. Rella flicked her ears back to her rider but the whites of her eyes showed as she threw a crazed look past Balthazar's nose. Rearing up, she pawed the air before spinning around and bolting back up the trail, Helena gripping grimly to the saddle.

"Shit, why did she act that way, Balthazar?" Sera asked and shortened her reins. "We need to go after them!"

Balthazar stood frozen, ears straining forward, and stared into the underbrush in front of them.

"Balthazar? What's happening?" Sera had never seen a unicorn act the way Rella had; even the foals had more sense than the filly did in that moment. The fact that Balthazar wasn't answering her sent a chill racing through her body.

Something is very wrong.

Drawing her pistol, she loaded bullets into the magazine of her new weapon. Raising the handgun in readiness, she kept her finger off the trigger until she could see her target. As she studied the greenery, she noticed the onyx stones around the base of Balthazar's horn flash briefly and she wondered what magic he was weaving. The leaves rustled in a sudden breeze and curled back, shrinking and twisting, until they revealed the mythic that watched them. A wild unicorn met their gaze before lowering its horn, pointing it directly at Sera's heart.

CHAPTER SIX

Confused, Sera lowered the barrel slightly but kept her finger near the trigger. The strange unicorn was a feral-looking thing, his matted mane hanging past his shoulders and his tail dragging on the ground. His coat was a deep sea-green, almost black, with scars chequering it. Leaves tangled through his mane and tail while sticky seedpods clung to his fetlocks.

"It is the king of my kind," Balthazar murmured, finally breaking his silence. He bowed low, touching his horn to the earth in a show of respect. Sera gripped the saddle with her hand and lowered her heels to keep from sliding forward onto his neck. She bobbed her head in deference to the king before Balthazar stood once more.

"I don't want your false allegiance," the Unicorn King addressed Balthazar with an angry snort, ignoring Sera. "How you have fallen, to allow a human to sit astride you." He tossed his mane in disgust.

"With all due respect, sire, the unicorns made a treaty with the humans."

"Not all of us agreed to that. It was an abomination to lower ourselves to become mere beasts of burden."

"It was a good decision. They offered us safety from those who would hunt us, easy access to food, and shelter from the elements."

"You've gone soft! You have become... domesticated." He spat the word out with such venom, it struck Sera like a blow. The unadulterated aggression that rolled off the unicorn in waves made her muscles tense as realisation struck.

Nothing we say will turn his thoughts. He won't be convinced that we live in mutual respect of each other.

Fear closed around her heart with an iron grip, standing the hairs on her arm to attention. She laid a cautionary hand against Balthazar's neck as she twisted in the saddle to search for any sign of Helena and Rella.

The king squealed and pawed the ground. "Don't think you're getting any help from your friends, I've sent them away."

"Dismount, Sera," her stallion commanded softly, intended for her ears only.

Without asking why, she did as he asked. Looking to Balthazar for guidance, she noticed his ears pinned against his head. Keeping her gun hand steady, she prepared to fight as she returned her attention to the mythic.

The green unicorn bared his teeth and hissed, "The time for talking has passed, colt. It is time for you to return to Ghaia's embrace. Perhaps the Goddess can show you the error of your ways."

"Get out of here, Seraphina!" Balthazar trumpeted to her.

"I'm not leaving you!" she shouted back, her finger hovering over the trigger.

"You must!" he whinnied, and leapt in front of her.

The king turned his head and pointed his horn at the nearest tree. Vines crept down the trunk, snaking towards Balthazar and Sera.

Eyes wide as she backed away, Sera asked, "What in the name of Ghaia is this?"

"This is his forest," grunted Balthazar. "The earth, the trees, the plants... they all submit to him. May the Four Gods help us."

With that, Balthazar plunged forward with a scream, his horn aimed at the king's heart. With a sweep of his horn, the other stallion parried with magic and struck Balthazar with a tree branch. Sera's unicorn fell heavily on his side, smashing his head on a rock. She screamed and dashed toward him, but was halted by the green unicorn advancing on her. The trees surrounding them leaned closer, the vines reaching their tendrils towards her. She raised her pistol once again and aimed at his heart, yet hesitated to fire. The king noticed her indecision and a puzzled look flashed over his face before he lowered his head and sent a blast of pure magic at her. She pulled the trigger at the same moment and something in the air between them shimmered and shattered. The intense magic the king had aimed at her split apart and warped. The power still blasted into her and threw her back, cracking her body into a trunk. The tree wrapped its boughs around her, holding her in place as he limped forward, his shoulder bleeding where her bullet had grazed his hide, the silvery liquid shining in the afternoon light.

"Stop. Please." She feebly held her hand up to put one last effort in to her survival, the tree's branches making it difficult to move even that much.

The king halted abruptly and stared at her palm, eyeing the golden scar. "What is th–"

His words were cut off when Balthazar rushed him from the side, smashing into his body. He stumbled, and Balthazar took the opportunity to swing his horn into the king's. It slid down the length, producing a screeching sound that put Sera's teeth on edge. The buckskin stallion's horn glowed brightly before it suddenly sliced cleanly through the king's horn. A massive blast of magic radiated from the horn and the green unicorn screamed. An eerie breeze swept through the clearing and then everything fell unnaturally still. The tree holding Sera went limp and she managed to struggle free.

Balthazar knelt in front of her and demanded, "Get on, quickly!"

She snatched her pistol from the ground, avoiding the flailing king, and scrambled into the saddle, her back screaming in protest from where she'd struck the tree. As soon as she was mounted Balthazar galloped away, leaving the king of the unicorns writhing on the ground as his magic leaked away.

A few minutes later, Balthazar slowed to a walk. Sera's gut roiled and she focused on keeping her lunch down as she relived the disturbing scene. Squeezing her eyes shut briefly, she whispered in quiet horror, "Balthazar... what did you do to him?"

"It was you or him, Seraphina. I couldn't..." his voice hitched, "I couldn't bear it if I lost another rider. I had to choose you."

Still tormented by the image of the mythic losing his magic, she stroked her unicorn's neck and murmured, "Thank you for saving me."

But at what cost?

Balthazar nickered low in his throat in response to her gratitude. The trees were back in their uniform lines now, giving Sera hope Helena and Rella weren't too far away. Biting her lip to keep from crying out from the pain wracking her body, she fumbled in the pouch on her belt and pulled out the container marked Heal. Scooping a dab onto her hand, she rubbed it on her back as best as she could. Before she could tell Balthazar to stop so she could put some on his head wound, he stumbled un-expectedly and fell to his knees, throwing Sera forward. She curled into a ball and managed to roll as she fell. Her back flared in pain as she hit the earth, pine needles softening her landing. Slowly pushing herself onto her hands and knees, she breathed deeply, pushing the pain away. Raising her eyes, she cried out when she realised Balthazar was unconscious.

CHAPTER SEVEN

"NO, NO, NO, COME on Balthazar. You need to wake up!" she cried as she crawled to him and ran her hands over his head, noting the silver blood that had congealed on the wound from where his skull had struck the rock. Pulling her phone out, she checked if she had any signal and released a little sigh of relief when she saw the two bars in the top corner. She brought up the contact details for the MRO and called the front desk.

"Thank you for calling the Mythic Relations Office, how can–"

"It's Tracker Seraphina, I need you to put me through to Tracker Helena's personal mobile," Sera interrupted.

"I'm sorry, she's out on a training run but I can leave a message for her."

"She's out on the training run with me and we've been separated. I need to be put through to her now!"

"Right away, please hold the line." There was a dialling sound then the phone rang.

"Tracker Helena speaking." Sera had never been so happy to hear the Head Tracker's voice.

"Helena, it's Sera, are you okay?"

"Yes, Rella only just stopped bolting a few minutes ago. I couldn't get through to her. Are you two okay?"

"No, we had a fight with the Unicorn King and Balthazar saved us, but now he's passed out."

Helena cursed. "Stay where you are and set the GPS beacon going on your PSB. I'll find you."

Tapping the screen of her Personal Security Band, she set the emergency signal going. *Thank Ghaia I decided to upgrade it to include the safety feature. I didn't want a repeat of getting lost, but I didn't expect I would need to use it this soon.*

Sera grabbed the Heal container that had fallen out of her hands when she was thrown and scraped the last of it onto Balthazar's head wound. Checking him over for any other obvious injuries, she was relieved to find none. His breathing remained steady as she watched the flesh knit back together on his skull, but he didn't wake up. A few minutes later Sera heard a distinct three-beat rhythm and shortly after Helena and Rella appeared, cantering towards them.

"What in the name of Ghaia happened?" Helena demanded as she leapt from Rella's back and rushed to Balthazar's side. She ran her hands over his still form while she listened.

Sera gave a helpless shrug and explained as succinctly as she could. "The king of the unicorns and Balthazar had an argument about the treaty and he rejected the notion of bearing a rider. He attacked us and Balthazar tried to protect me but the king used his magic to strike him with a tree branch. When he hit the ground he cracked his head on a rock. I managed to distract the king long enough for Balthazar to regain consciousness and attack him. He..." she sucked in a shuddering breath at the traumatising memory before continuing, "destroyed the king's horn." Both Helena and Rella gasped at the revelation. "There was an explosion of magic and we ran away. We only made it this far before he collapsed. I've put some Heal on his injuries but he's not waking up." Her breath hitched as sobs threatened to overwhelm her.

"Shit," exclaimed Helena and clasped her hands together, worry marring her features.

Rella stepped forward and leant down. "It's my fault he was alone. It is my duty to heal him."

"It wasn't your fault, Rella," insisted Sera. "The king told us he had sent you away. You couldn't have ignored his magic, he was too powerful."

Rella's big brown eyes regarded Sera and she blinked slowly. "Be that as it may, I must heal him." She took a deep breath and pointed her horn at the unconscious buckskin stallion. Slowly, she advanced and, dropping to her knees, pierced his hide. The amber stones shone as she drove her horn into his chest, towards his heart. Sera cried out and rushed to stop her but Helena grabbed her around the waist and held her back.

"Just wait. This is the only way."

"What's she doing?" Sera yelled, fighting to pull away. "She'll kill him!"

Helena used the same soothing tone she'd used on Rella earlier. "Let her do what must be done. When a unicorn is exposed to that much raw magic, they can die unless the power is filtered by another magic user. It is likely they will both be unwell for a few days, but they should survive it."

Sera stopped struggling and watched in horror as green light drained from Balthazar's body and was absorbed into Rella's horn. The filly shuddered but maintained her position, her horn lodged deep in his chest as the magic was transferred. Sweat glistened on her chestnut coat and she panted from the effort. Once her entire body was trembling, she withdrew her horn and collapsed to the ground beside Balthazar, the hole in his chest healing immediately.

Eyes closed, she murmured, "I'm sorry I can't do more."

The stallion stirred and slowly opened his eyes. Sitting up with a groan, he looked at Rella lying beside him, dropped his nose to his chest and snorted at the healed wound. "It seems I owe you a great debt, young one."

She smiled weakly and whispered, "You'd do the same for me."

Sera interrupted by crawling to Balthazar and hugging his neck tightly. "I thought I'd lost you."

"I will be fine now. There is no need to fret."

Sera wiped the tears from her eyes and gave him a weak smile. "It seems you have another being you owe your life to." Turning to the chestnut filly, she winked and said, "Don't let him forget that he owes you. He'll do just about anything to get out of your debt."

Balthazar chuffed in amusement and rolled his eyes. "Thank you for that, Sera. Now I owe my life to both of you. I can only hope that Rella is better at counting than you are. I'm fairly sure I've saved you seven times now. So, I'm winning."

Rella opened her eyes long enough to cast a bewildered look at them as they chuckled together.

"Sorry to interrupt the comedy show," Helena's voice was tart, "but I need you to focus. After I got your call, I contacted the MRO and asked a Hunter to join us. We need to bring the rogue unicorn in for questioning. I understand it's been a shock, but do you think you can guide Hunter Tyler to where you left the king?"

A chill crept over her skin at the mention of Tyler's name but she pushed it aside and nodded, bound to her duty. "Do you really think we need to bring him in, Helena?"

She squinted her eyes shrewdly in Sera's direction. "But Sera, he's gone rogue. Shouldn't he be brought to justice for attacking a human?"

Sera narrowed her eyes at the older Tracker, trying to comprehend the underlying question the woman was insinuating. "He hurt Balthazar because he was protecting me, but the king barely touched me. In any case, he isn't a threat anymore because he lost his magic when his horn shattered. What's the point? If we do bring him in, shouldn't we be helping to heal him as best we can, not sending him to the IRC?"

A smile flickered over Helena's lips and her eyes lit with a sharp fire. She opened her mouth to say something but cut herself off and turned her head towards the city. Sera heard it then too, the distant sound of hoofbeats, softened by the pine needles.

Helena leaned forward and grasped Sera's shoulders firmly and whispered hurriedly, "You need to visit the nest of the Little Birds." Casting a quick glance over her shoulder, she brought a hand to her neck and pulled out her necklace where a tiny wooden carving of a bird hung. Lifting it over her head, she shoved it at Sera and hissed, "Look for their sign and give them this. Tell them Wolfseye sent you. Don't breathe a word to anyone else."

Before Sera could ask Helena anything else, she rose swiftly to her feet and turned to greet Hunter Tyler on his unicorn, Madatrax. Sera furtively pulled the necklace over her head, stuffing the wooden bird under her collar, and joined the Head Tracker.

CHAPTER EIGHT

"Tracker Helena." Tyler nodded respectfully. He smiled warmly at Sera. "Tracker Seraphina. It looks like you've seen some action today. I hope you're not hurt."

He dismounted smoothly from his grey unicorn and gave her a hug. She remained stiff and shot him a cold look when his hand stayed around her waist a little longer than necessary. He hid a chuckle, unperturbed by her chilly reception. Eyeing the two unicorns that still lay on the ground, he raised a questioning eyebrow.

Helena explained briefly what had happened and added, "I've asked Tracker Seraphina to lead you to the location of the fight and to see whether you can find the rogue unicorn. He may be king of his kind, but he still answers to our laws. Try not to hurt him any more than he already has been."

Tyler bobbed his head and leapt onto Madatrax's back before offering his hand to Sera. Stifling a grimace, she begrudgingly accepted his help and mounted the unicorn. Her back protested as she twisted to sit behind the saddle, but the pain had subsided somewhat thanks to the Heal cream.

"Report directly to me when you're back. I'll get these unicorns to the stables, then return to the MRO. Call me if you need back-up." Helena caught and held Sera's gaze and said, "Good luck." Sera knew she wasn't talking about this mission.

"Thank you, ma'am!" Tyler replied and kicked the grey stallion straight into a canter. The sudden lunge forward nearly unseated Sera but she grabbed Tyler's waist to steady herself until she found the unicorn's rhythm.

"It's nice to feel your arms around me," he threw over his shoulder glibly.

Everything about his smug countenance grated on Sera. With a grimace, she released her hold on him and sat tall, allowing her hips to sway with each stride. She'd rather take her chances of falling off than give Tyler the satisfaction of her touch. He chuckled briefly at her rebellion but shortly turned businesslike.

"So, Tracker Helena gave me a quick overview, but what else do I need to know about the unicorn we're hunting?"

That was the one good thing about Tyler, he was a decent Hunter and could be relied on to get the job done and keep her safe. From the rogue mythics anyway.

"He was against the Peace Covenant and challenged Balthazar for protecting me and accepting our laws. He had powerful magic and took control of the surrounding environment to fight us. But I think his power was stripped when Balthazar attacked him and..." she gritted her teeth and pushed through the churning in her stomach, "broke his horn."

"Wow! I didn't know that was possible." Tyler's voice had an eerie edge to it that she found even more disturbing than usual.

"It was horrible," she said sharply, hoping to force him to consider the disablement as seriously as she was.

"Of course, it must have been a terrible thing to see," he agreed hastily. "Do you think you can get us back to where you fought him?"

"Yes, I think so. Keep following this path for now, and once the plantation ends and the wilds take over you should see our trail through the bushes on your left."

"It seems you might be getting in on the action more than usual today," he teased and tugged on the reins, slowing Madatrax to a brisk walk.

She scowled. "I'm not a fan. I track. You hunt. I'm not cut out for combat."

They rode on in silence and Sera reflected on the fight. Pushing her horror aside, she analysed the actions of the mythic. *He obviously held strong beliefs about the Peace Covenant. Balthazar and I represented everything he hated about what happened to his kind. He shouldn't have attacked us, but I suppose we did invade his turf. I do have to do my job, but it doesn't feel right to capture him. Especially now that he's injured.*

Interrupting her thoughts, Tyler reached a hand back and rubbed her thigh, letting his fingers trail up the seam of her trousers. She gritted her teeth and growled, "Stop it."

"But babycakes," he turned in the saddle so he could see her, "it's just us. No need to be embarrassed. I know you want it."

"You know I don't," she spat out and prepared to leap off Madatrax.

"Don't you dare," Tyler snarled and grabbed her shirt, pinching her skin through the fabric. "I've been patient. If you're a good girl, I will continue to be. If you test me, I will fuck you, whether you want it or not."

Dread filled her soul and she stilled. Glaring at him, she prayed the hatred she harboured was obvious in her eyes.

He smirked and squeezed her leg before facing forward once more. "Good girl."

Pushing the queasy feeling in her stomach aside, she gestured to the left, thankful for the distraction. "Just here. Please be as quiet as you can, Madatrax."

The unicorn snorted his acquiescence and moved silently through the bushes. The trail was easy to follow, broken branches and flattened grass marking their wild dash like a neon sign. The air was still and heavy, making them all sweat. A few minutes later, she whispered, "I'll hop down and do some recon before we get to the clearing in case he's still there."

Tyler nodded and jerked Madatrax to a halt before pulling his pistol out of its holster and loading the bullets. Sera slid down the unicorn's side and landed softly on a patch of moss. Moving quietly, she stayed low and circled off the path, carefully sweeping leaves away from her face as she slipped through the underbrush. The dappled sunlight that pierced the treetops was waning as the sun commenced its descent towards the horizon. She placed each foot down cautiously as the clearing came into view. Peering through a gap in the foliage she saw the tree that had held her as the king of the unicorns advanced. The tree and the grass in that section were burnt black and looked as if a bomb had exploded, sweeping everything outward from the centre. A pool of silver liquid stained the ground and Sera flinched as she realised it was the king's blood. Droplets lay a clear path into the trees on the opposite side of Sera's location.

She whistled low, her signal to Tyler that all was safe, and stepped slowly into the open. Keeping her senses alert, she followed the trail of unicorn blood into the forest. She felt rather than heard Madatrax and Tyler following her at an innocuous distance. Even in the dim light of dusk, other signs of the injured unicorn's flight were obvious as she tracked him. Hoof prints in the soft earth, green strands of his mane where it had caught on a branch, as well as the slowly thinning droplets of blood led her down a shallow gulley to a creek. She slowed, and waited for Tyler to catch up.

Readying her pistol, she whispered, "I think he's close. He slowed to a walk when he reached the stream, and this last patch of blood is still warm. Be prepared. He may not have magic, but if he isn't unconscious he'll be wild with pain."

Tyler nodded silently and dismounted.

Together, the three of them waded into the knee-deep water and fanned out, weapons ready, while Madatrax's silver stones encircling his horn glowed as he conjured a ward. A light breeze flurried around them and offered some relief from the humidity. There was a massive boulder on the bank that hung over the creek in front of them, blocking their view of the riverbed as it swept around the corner created by the rock.

Sera glanced at Tyler and said grimly, "I've got a bad feeling about this."

His mouth thinned and he raised his pistol, finger hovering beside the trigger. They rounded the corner together and Sera gasped while Tyler cursed at the grisly sight that met them. The king was dead. The green unicorn lay on a rock in the middle of the creek but his body had been torn apart. The last of his blood was seeping into the water, creating a rainbow sheen on the surface. His belly had been sliced open and his organs torn out and thrown haphazardly around his body. Sera leant over with her hands on her knees and retched at the slaughter, and Madatrax pinned his ears back and trumpeted his horror to the empty skies.

"Who could have done this?" mused Tyler as he swept the area, searching for the assailant.

The wind changed direction and the cloying scent of decay suddenly rolled over the group. A heavy splash sounded from behind them and a strange voice answered, "Me."

CHAPTER NINE

THEY SPUN AROUND TO face the threat and were greeted with the leering smile of a harpy. The eerily beautiful face and torso of a woman sat atop the feathered rump of a vulture, with dark wings tucked close to her back. Her black hair hung limply over pointed ears and covered her breasts.

"Seraphina! How nice to see you again," the harpy rasped as her oily feathers dripped black blood into the water, the stain spreading downstream.

Tyler shot a confused look towards Sera which she mirrored with an equally puzzled expression. Meeting the harpy's gaze, she spat out, "I don't recognise you, harpy. Why did you mutilate the Unicorn King?"

The harpy grinned, her human face twisting as she bared her sharp teeth. "Ah. So, he did erase your memory after all. I wondered."

Sera took a step back in shock, before demanding, "What do you know? Who erased my memory?"

The harpy tsked and wagged a finger in her direction. "A harpy never reveals her secrets. I must thank you for your help in weakening that sad excuse of a king, it made my job a lot easier."

"Don't thank me! I had nothing to do with it!" Sera's throat burned from the harpy's toxic insinuation.

"You sure about that?" The harpy winked, her purple irises almost glowing in her almond-shaped eyes. Another nauseating wave of decay assaulted their noses.

"It wasn't my fault," she snarled.

The harpy cocked her head with a sly look and said, "To be honest, Seraphina, I did him a favour. What kind of quality of life would he have had without his horn? Disabled, the loss of his crown, ostracised from his kind, unable to access the magic that has been part of his life for a century. Letting him live would have been cruel."

Her mouth twisted at the truth in the words but Sera didn't let the harpy distract her. "Why did you do it?"

"It was nothing personal. I have a job to do and I did it. You weren't supposed to find me, though. You're lucky that my employer still wants you alive, Seraphina." She paused and tapped her chin with long nails as she considered the Hunter and his unicorn. "As for your friends, though... I suppose I had better clean this mess up."

She launched herself at Madatrax, her talons outstretched and wings beating fast to raise her above his head. He reared and greeted her attack with grim satisfaction as he pawed the air, aiming to strike a heavy blow. While this was happening, Sera and Tyler aimed their handguns and released a steady barrage of bullets, only stopping to reload. The harpy was lightning fast though and danced through the air, avoiding hooves and bullets easily. Realising his tactic wasn't working, Madatrax dropped down to all four hooves. The splash of water caught the last of the sunlight, looking like tiny fire crystals suspended in the air. Tyler's unicorn spun his glowing horn in a circle, sending a miniature hurricane towards the harpy. With a powerful beat of her wings, she thrust herself away and avoided the worst of the wind. The magical hurricane petered out into the dusky sky as

Madatrax aimed his horn at her heart. Before he could release the rising magic, the harpy bared her teeth in a maniacal smile before sweeping her wings wide and sending a series of sharp-edged feathers at the Hunter and his unicorn. They cried out and tried to shield themselves from the attack. Madatrax threw a ward up in front of Tyler but not soon enough to stop all the blades. Lacerations criss-crossed both their bodies and Tyler swore. Sera watched helplessly as the harpy continued her waltz through the air, easily avoiding the attacks they sent her way.

The harpy giggled, a sickening sound, and announced, "I tire of these games. Enough." She closed her eyes and held her thin arms high, her clawed hands palm-up, and uttered a strange guttural croak. Both the Hunter and his unicorn fell limp, splashing into the creek, the whites of their eyes showing as they convulsed.

Suddenly, a large blur of grey streaked from the darkening sky and crashed into the harpy. She screamed and opened her eyes to face the new attacker. With the body of a horse and the head and wings of an eagle, the hippogryph's momentum drove her to the ground near Sera, where he began pummelling her with his hooves and snapping at her face with his sharp beak. Sera lined her eye up with the sight, waiting for an opportunity to fire without hitting the hippogryph. The harpy's purple irises pulsed with a light from within and she screamed in the hippogryph's face, ignoring his attack. He flew backwards and landed in a crumpled heap in the stream, washing a wave over the still forms of Tyler and Madatrax.

Sera squeezed the trigger, sending another bullet towards the harpy. This one finally found its mark. The harpy screamed as it buried into the flesh of her shoulder.

Holding her arm as the thick black blood dripped down her pale skin, she turned to Sera with murder in her eyes. Just as Sera pulled the trigger again, a black lynx leapt out of the bushes and pounced on the harpy, driving her into the ground. Sera had no idea how her second bullet missed both of them. The lynx snarled, his fangs inches from the harpy's throat. The black flames that circled his neck and ran along his spine flared high and Sera smelt the harpy's burning flesh. She screamed at him, but her magic didn't affect the lynx.

She turned her face away from him and locked eyes with Sera, hissing, "He has plans for you. There is no escaping him." With that, she glowed brightly and vanished from beneath the lynx's large paws. He roared his rage at losing his quarry and swiped the ground, leaving gashes in the earth. Sera looked around frantically but there was no sign of the harpy. The hippogryph rose from the stream and shook himself, water droplets shimmering in the waning moon's light. Carefully using his beak, he propped Madatrax's head onto a rock to keep his muzzle out of the water, then dragged the unconscious body of Tyler onto the bank.

Approaching Sera, the grey hippogryph lowered his head and asked, "Are you all right, my sweet?"

"Where... where did she go?" she stammered.

"The harpy transported herself to safety," the lynx explained.

Sinking to her knees, her body shaking from the adrenaline, she lowered her head into her hands. The hippogryph approached and shoved his beak against her cheek, nuzzling her.

"My sweet Seraphina. Are you all right?" he asked again.

She yelped and raised her face abruptly. "How do you know my name?"

The hippogryph's beak hung open in shock. "It's me. Torvold. Don't you remember me?"

The lynx was watching with interest as confusion played out on Sera's face. Before she could respond, he sniffed the air and announced coolly, "Her memory has been wiped. But only for the time she was with Arius until she returned to Mandar City. That is a clever bit of magic. How interesting." He said it all matter-of-factly as he sat on his haunches and observed her reaction.

"Who's Arius? And who are you both?" she asked, feeling more confused than ever.

"She's forgotten Arius?" the hippogryph – Torvold – screeched. "How is that possible?"

"Do shut up, feather-head," the lynx growled. "If you throw too much information at her, her brain will implode and she'll be no use to anyone."

"But... but, they're Soulbo—"

"I said, shut up," he interrupted with a snarl to emphasise his point.

"Fine," Torvold snapped. "Can we at least tell her who we are?"

The black cat cocked his head and scrutinised her. Baring his teeth in a foreign grin, he purred, "I don't think she'll let us leave if we don't divulge something."

CHAPTER TEN

THE HIPPOGRYPH SWUNG AROUND to look into Sera's eyes, letting his tail swing so it hit the lynx who growled his annoyance. "I'm Torvold, but you used to call me Tor. We met through a friend..." he paused and looked at the lynx for approval.

"I assume it's this Arius fellow?" Sera interjected.

Tor chortled and nodded. "Yes. We met through Arius. A lot happened, and I'm not supposed to tell you too much apparently," he shot a glare at his friend, "but there was a storm and you and Arius were separated. You crashed into my flock's nest and after some... negotiations with my mother, I chose to help guide you back to Arius. But you were stolen away by that harpy and we couldn't find you."

"Right." She gave him a bland look. "Now I'm more confused than ever." He shrugged his blue-grey wings apologetically. She turned her attention to the lynx. "And who are you, and how do we know each other?"

"We've met twice but I never told you my name."

Tor poked his tongue out at the lynx before saying, "His name is Idris. He will talk you around in circles and never get around to introducing himself." The black cat swatted the hippogryph with his tail. "What? It's true. You're a terrible conversationalist."

Ignoring Tor's jibe, Idris turned to Sera and said, "You need to get your memories back. There is change coming and you need to know what you're in for."

"I mean, it's a good plan. But how in the Four Gods' names am I supposed to do that?" she asked drily.

He studied her for a moment and then said cryptically, "That is something you need to figure out alone."

"Which means he doesn't know," Tor said with a chuckle.

"You are a vexing creature," Idris proclaimed.

"I do try," came Tor's smug response with a fluff of his feathers. Turning serious, he said, "Sera, we are here to help you however we can. But unfortunately, Idris is right. You need your memories back. I don't know how you can do that, but you'll have to figure something out."

"I don't understand why you can't just tell me," she complained bitterly.

I finally have access to the answers to what happened and they won't explain anything!

Sorry, but it's for the best.

Sera started at the foreign voice in her head, her jaw dropping. *What in Ghaia's name is happening? Am I going crazy?*

The lynx grinned at her. *I can hear your thoughts, silly girl.*

Tor unknowingly interrupted their silent conversation and exclaimed, "Talk to the cat! I'd tell you everything in a heartbeat!"

The lynx rolled his eyes at the hippogryph before turning his steady amber gaze on Sera, and spoke aloud. "I understand your frustration. Both of us were only spectators to part of your story. But if we tell you everything that we witnessed, you either wouldn't believe us, or we would damage your mind as you try to marry the truth with the missing pieces of your memory. Trust me when I say, it's better this way."

Sera sighed heavily, frustration overtaking all other emotions.

Tor stepped closer to her and said, "I do have something that might make you feel better. When you—" he hesitated when Idris shot him a sharp look before continuing, "returned to the city, you left this behind." He bowed his head and, using his beak, undid a leather pouch attached to his foreleg. Laying the pouch on the ground, he flicked the leather open and pulled a blade out.

"Firinne!" Sera cried and snatched up her lost knife. "Thank you so much, Tor! I thought I'd lost it forever." She gripped the staghorn handle tightly and a sense of ease washed over her. It felt as if a part of her arm had been missing and was now reattached.

"You're welcome, my sweet." Tor's eyes crinkled happily.

The lynx massaged his claws into the earth, gouging small furrows into the dirt as his tail twitched in agitation. "I too have a gift for you that may help you on your journey to accessing your memories." Idris padded to the stream and gazed into the water before opening his mouth wide and roaring.

Tor glanced at Sera and chuckled at her quizzical look. "Your guess is as good as mine, my sweet."

Idris placed a black paw against the dark surface of the creek and the water stilled. A perfect circle of water rose into the air in front of him. Its shape wobbled and morphed as it shimmered in the moonlight before it flattened into an oval the size of her palm and, under the direction of the lynx, lowered onto a small rock on the bank. The water nestled into the stone, carving the centre of the rock away to create a shallow vessel. There was a flash of bright light as it sealed itself to the newly-made bowl. Idris nodded to her, signalling the magic was complete, so she stepped forward and picked it up. The rock fit into her palm neatly while the water had solidified so it didn't move as she twisted the bowl around. Gently touching the surface, she found it to be hard, like glass.

"How did you do that?" she whispered in awe.

"Magic." Tor snorted at Idris' simplified explanation. The lynx's fiery mane flared higher, and he bared his teeth at Tor. "Fine. It was a complicated spell that required a little bit of help from another magic wielder."

"That's amazing. Thank you," she murmured as she weighed it carefully in her hands, surprised at how light it was.

"It's not from me," he replied. "An old friend wished for you to have it."

"Who?" she asked.

The lynx opened his mouth to answer, but Tor interrupted with a glare. "I know that look. For Ghaia's sake, just give her a straight answer, Idris."

The feline mythic sighed and replied, "You ruin all my fun, Torvold." He turned back to Sera and begrudgingly said, "It's from your grandmother."

Sera gasped at the revelation and held it up, letting the light from the moon catch it and cast patterns over the surface of the solid water.

Why does Nanna want me to have this?

Tor mirrored her thoughts and asked, "It's pretty and all, but what's it actually for?"

"Your grandmother found a Seeing Pool. I owed her a favour, so together we managed to combine our magic to teleport a sample of the water through this stream to you."

Sera's mouth hung open. "What? This is water from a Seeing Pool? As in, the Seeing Pool that shows the past, present and future? That's insane! Hang on..." she whipped her head around to stare at the lynx. "Did you say my nanna used magic? That's not possible! Only mythics can access magic." Staring at the bowl of solid water, she murmured low, speaking more to herself than the mythics, "I mean, people call her a witch, but she's just extremely talented at alchemy."

"It's not my secret to tell. I will leave it up to Del to explain where her power comes from. The Seeing Stone you have there does not have the same level of power that you would experience from the Seeing Pool. But we hope you can gain glimpses of insight from it that will help guide you on your path." The lynx flicked an ear towards Tyler as he stirred. "That's our cue to leave. Maybe don't mention us to your friends when they wake up. We will meet again, Seraphina. Good luck."

Tor rushed forward and swept a wing around Sera, pulling her into his feathery chest in a hug. "Good to see you again, my sweet. Hopefully, next time we meet you'll have full recollection of how charming and helpful I am." He winked at her before cantering a few strides and leaping into the air, beating his wings vigorously to rise above the treetops.

Sera looked to see which way the lynx was headed, but Idris had already melted into the cover of the forest. She glanced down at her Seeing Stone and caught the flash of an emerald eye in its depths. She sucked in a breath and stared into the solidified water, desperate to see it again, but only the stony bottom met her gaze.

Tyler groaned and sat up, holding his head in his hands. Sera shoved the stone into the back pocket of her trousers and knelt in front of him.

"Are you badly hurt?" she asked him, more out of duty than actual concern.

"I think I'm okay. A cracking headache and some cuts," he bit out as he assessed the damage to his body. He leaned on Sera's shoulder and stood with a groan. She stepped out from under his arm as soon as he remained steady on his feet. Holding a hand to his temple, he asked, "What happened?"

"The harpy used her magic to send you both unconscious." Sera's mind raced for a plausible explanation of how she saved them. "I managed to graze her with a bullet while she was focused on her attack and I think the shock of the pain distracted her enough to stop her spell. Her eyes glowed purple and then she vanished into thin air." Sera shook her head. "I've never seen anything like it."

"She said she knew you," he asked her, eyebrows drawn together.

"I swear to you, I have no recollection of the harpy. But my guess is that maybe I met her during the time that I lost my memory. That's the only reason I can think of how she recognised me."

"Hmmm." He gave her a funny look but left her on the bank and limped to Madatrax.

"I'll ring Tracker Helena, okay?" she called after him.

"Yep," Tyler called over his shoulder as he took the MRO Survival Kit from the saddle bag attached to his unicorn and pulled out the container of Heal.

As Sera waited for Helena to answer, she watched Tyler layer his own body with the ointment before attending to the stallion's injuries. Her mouth pulled down but before she could say anything, the Head Tracker answered.

"What's happened, Tracker Seraphina?"

"Something terrible."

CHAPTER ELEVEN

SERA LAY IN BED, watching the late morning sunlight dapple through her curtains. Tracker Helena had insisted she take the rest of the week off to recover from yesterday's fight with the harpy. The Head Tracker had sent another Tracker out today to see if they could find any signs of where the rogue mythic had disappeared to, but Sera doubted they would find anything. She groaned as she rolled over, not physically exhausted so much as mentally drained from the events of yesterday. Picking up the Seeing Stone from her bedside table, she stared at it, hoping for some flash of insight. When nothing happened, she sighed and dropped it on her pillow, then grabbed her phone and checked for any new messages before calling the stable master.

"Hey, Jor, I was just checking in to see how Balthazar is doing today?" Placing the phone on speaker, she examined the Seeing Stone again.

"That's sweet of you, Tracker Seraphina," replied the middle-aged woman. "He's fine. Exhausted but recovering well. So is Rella. I'll tell him you were asking after him."

"Tell him I'm sorry I can't get there today," she said while she absentmindedly turned the Seeing Stone over in her hands and rubbed her fingers over the glossy surface.

"I'm sure he'll understand. It sounds as if you have your own battles to recover from."

"How do you know about that?" Sera asked.

"You know how word gets around the MRO," she replied dismissively. "I can't chat, sorry, I'm preparing the three-year-olds for the Choosing on the weekend. It's a madhouse here."

"Okay, no problem. Thanks for answering my call, Jor."

"You're welcome. I'll be in touch if anything changes, but Balthazar is strong. He'll be fine. Cheerio!"

"Okay, bye then," she whispered and the stable master hung up. Tears pricked her eyes, but she wasn't sure if they were from relief, realising that her unicorn was going to survive, or from the overload of information she had learnt yesterday. Dropping the useless stone back on her pillow, Sera curled into a ball and pulled the sheets over her head. Darkness corrupted her thoughts and she couldn't find a scrap of joy in her soul. Her life was spiralling out of control and there was nothing she could do to stop it.

What if I never get my memory back? Is this how I'm going to feel for the rest of my life?

A shudder rippled over her skin as she considered the bleak future that awaited her.

What's the point of living if this is all that's left?

An invisible weight crushed her chest, squeezing her lungs tight. Her breaths came in sharp gulps as she strained for oxygen. Her heart raced, as if trying to fit a life's-worth of beats into the next minute while depression flooded her mind. A feral cry ripped from her throat and the tears she'd been holding back spilled onto her pillow. Unexpectedly, her mattress bounced slightly as Hazel's cat leapt onto her bed. Perry crept between her sheets and nestled against her back, purring loudly.

The comforting presence of the usually unfriendly tabby soothed the ragged edges of the hole in her heart. The panic attack that had threatened to overcome her receded and she drank in a deep lungful of air as the band around her chest eased. Each inhale left her a little lighter. Rolling onto her back, she warily scratched Perry behind the ears.

"Thank you," she whispered hoarsely.

He blinked at her once before jumping to the floor.

I can do this. I can be strong. I will find a way to get my memories back.

Swinging her legs out of bed, she brushed the tears from her cheeks. As she went to stand, a shimmer of light from the Seeing Stone caught her attention. She picked it up from where she'd dropped it on her pillow and stared into its glassy surface. The shallow bowl melded itself comfortably into her palm, as if it had been made to fit her hand. While she watched, clouds swirled in the centre before the image settled on a cave. She was looking at it as if she were caged inside the skeleton of some monstrous beast.

I wonder if this is a vision of the past or the future?

Small shapes flitted around her in the image, and she tilted the Seeing Stone in an attempt to understand what they were. She realised a colony of night scamps were attacking. Many of the large-eared, sharp-toothed mythics already lay dead on the ground but there were dozens more to take their place. As she watched the horrific battle a burst of flames ripped through the scene. Squeaking in fright, she jerked and fumbled the stone, dropping it to the floor. Snatching it back up, she looked to see where the fire had come from, but only empty stone stared back at her. The vision had faded. Sera cursed and shook the Seeing Stone, willing it to return. Nothing changed. Dropping her shoulders in defeat, she sighed heavily. Summoning her motivation, she forced herself to pull on a fresh set of jeans and a loose-fitting shirt, before tucking the Seeing Stone securely into her pocket.

Following Perry out of her tiny bedroom to the kitchen, she noticed a piece of paper on the island bench beside a pot of coffee and a plate of toast.

"Hey Sera, I wasn't sure what time you were going to wake up, but I made you breakfast anyway. I'll come home for lunch to check how you're doing. Text me if you need anything. Hazel xx"

She smiled at her friend's thoughtfulness and reached for the coffee. The pot was cold and she frowned. Sera glanced at the clock and was surprised to see that it was almost midday already. At that moment, she heard the control panel buzz on the front door and Hazel let herself in.

"Oh good, you're up! How're you feeling?" Hazel rushed over and gave Sera a hug. Without waiting for an answer, she pulled out two containers of pasta and shoved one towards Sera.

Sera's mouth watered as she breathed in the scent of basil in the bolognaise. "Thank you so much." She hugged her friend again. "I'm famished. This is perfect."

Hazel blushed and muttered, "It's no big deal." She pulled a chair out from the small dining table for Sera before moving to the opposite side and sitting down to eat. An audible grumble came from Sera's stomach, and she grinned sheepishly before digging into her pasta. While she stuffed her mouth, Hazel ate slowly, watching her with a peculiar expression.

Pausing her scoffing, Sera asked around a mouthful of food, "Mmph, what is it?"

"Life was already difficult for you, Sera. And then, after yesterday's events, it's all just gotten crazier. I can see you suffering. So, I was thinking about what helps me when my mental health is declining. And — hear me out — I really think it would help for you to go to Temple."

Sera leant back in her chair with a scowl and said, "That's your thing, Hazel."

"It might make you feel better," Hazel implored, her warm brown eyes looking even larger behind her glasses, making it difficult to say no. "And, of course, I'll come with you."

Sera screwed up her nose. "But you know I hate Temple." It was one of the few things they disagreed about. Hazel believed wholeheartedly in the Four Gods. Sera was undecided on their existence but had accepted a long time ago that if they did exist, they cared little for mortals.

"Ghaia's Temple is so peaceful. It always leaves me feeling grounded."

Sera sniggered and asked, "Please tell me that wasn't a pun? The Earth Goddess' Temple leaves you feeling grounded? Really?"

Hazel flashed an impetuous smile that lit up her face and said, "I do love a good pun. But sadly no, that wasn't intentional. I'm not that witty."

"You're plenty witty," Sera mumbled whilst polishing off her lunch. "Fine. I'll go. But I reserve the right to leave if it gets too much."

Her friend darted around the table to her and squeezed her in an awkward side hug. "Thank you. At the very least it won't cause any harm, and with any luck, it will help you. Why don't we go now?"

Sera snorted drily. "You want to strike while the werewolf is still howling, huh?"

"Can't give you a chance to come up with an excuse to get out of it." Hazel smirked and winked.

"What about work? Your lunch break is nearly over."

"I spoke to my boss and he let me take the rest of the day off." She grinned wickedly. "I told him I had some final details to tie up in preparation for the Choosing. Which isn't a lie. I'll just do it after Temple."

"Fine." Sera groaned in defeat. "I give up. Seeing as you've got an answer for everything."

Hazel clapped her hands together gleefully. "Come on, get your shoes on and let's go! I'll bring something for the offering from both of us."

Sera groaned again. *I already regret this decision.*

CHAPTER TWELVE

THE TEMPLE WAS THE oldest building Sera had seen in Mandar City. The pillars were crumbling in places where the vines had tried to reclaim it. The massive building sat in the middle of a garden, with native trees dotting the lawn and meandering paths threading between flowering shrubs. The tinkle of a brook reached her ears as they entered through the wrought-iron gates. Sera felt as if a veil had been lifted to a time before the Mythic War. The Mandar City that she knew was a geometric maze of concrete. Ghaia's Temple was all soft edges, arches and filled with nature. She let out a long breath that she felt she had been holding onto for weeks now.

Hazel noticed and graced her with a brilliant smile. "I told you it would help," the brown-haired girl whispered as she nudged her with an elbow, eyebrow raised in triumph. Sera rolled her eyes but linked her arm through Hazel's as they walked up the stairs to the massive wooden door. Together, they stepped into the shadow of Ghaia's Temple.

Studying the mottled texture of the main door's timber, Sera let go of her friend and allowed her fingertips to trail over the grain before hurrying to follow Hazel inside the Temple. She always claimed she was too busy or exhausted to attend the services held at the Goddess' temple, but the truth was, she didn't know how much faith she put in the Four Gods. Ghaia for Earth, Bhelanos for Fire,

Caehli for Air and Aquera for Water. Her brows pulled together as she struggled to remember the location of the other Gods' Temples. Hazel had told her of the Temple for Caelhi in the snowy country of Soldenheim but she couldn't recall where the others were. She should probably find that out, but shrugged, dismissing the notion.

Does it really matter? Pretty sure I'm not planning on visiting them anytime soon.

As she traipsed after Hazel, Sera blinked, waiting for her eyes to grow accustomed to the dimness. Columns and stone statues of mythics lined the entire main hall and blossoming moonflowers that draped down from hanging pots perfumed the air. While their delicate white petals were lovely to look at, their cloying scent was too sweet, causing her nose to wrinkle and giving her an instant headache. An impressive carving of the Earth Goddess presided over the end of the hallway and Sera caught her breath as she admired the craftsmanship. The image of Ghaia had been recreated from an enormous living tree. Mythics must have helped produce this masterpiece since Sera had no doubt magic was involved in creating the living statue. Foliage cascaded around Ghaia's face like hair, and two large branches formed her arms that were opened wide in a welcoming pose. Her body morphed into the tree trunk but the roots were exposed, spreading to create the entrance and make way for the steps that led down into the inner sanctum of Ghaia's Temple.

An ominous feeling and a flash of black leathery wings flickered at the edge of Sera's vision and she swung around, hand ready to unsheathe Firinne, anxiously searching for the attacker. The image faded as quickly as it had come and she slowly relaxed out of her fighting stance.

Maybe yesterday's fight affected me more than I thought it did.

Mythics and humans moved through the impressive space, some leaving from prayer, others milling about and enjoying the beauty of the Earth Goddess' home in Mandar City. A constant low hum that melted into her bones echoed through the chamber, but she couldn't figure out where the noise came from. Before she could ask Hazel, a gluxxor caught their attention. Shivers prickled over her skin, and it wasn't just from the cool air of the Temple. The tall reptilian mythic stood on his rear legs and was clothed in a simple brown robe that rustled softly over his scaled skin as he bowed. His eyes remained closed while his scaled tail swept downward, making the bow more extravagant than expected.

"Welcome to Ghaia's Temple," he droned in a soothing monotone. "I am Brother Reikuul." His tongue flicked out over his snout, tasting the air. "Please do not take weapons into the inner sanctum. It is against Ghaia's teachings to possess a weapon in her presence."

Sera frowned and placed a protective hand on Firinne. She didn't intend on losing her blade ever again, and she wasn't sure she trusted this gluxxor. Glancing at Hazel, who nodded encouragingly, she pursed her lips, uneasy.

"Fine," she eventually ground out. Unsheathing the knife, she placed it hilt first into the gluxxor's waiting talons. "Where can I pick it up once we're finished?"

"I will ensure it is returned to you safely at the end of your visit, Tracker Seraphina."

She flinched. *How does he know my name?*

Hazel had walked ahead to place their offering of coffee beans, a sprig of rosemary and a small bunch of home-grown pansies beside Ghaia's statue on the offering table and didn't hear the exchange. Brother Reikuul held the blade tightly, drawing blood from the palm of his clawed hand, and opened his eyes. They were milky white and stared blindly at Sera as she cried out.

"What are you doing? You've hurt yourself, you silly fool! Let me get you some help."

She turned to call out to Hazel, but she was gone. They were completely alone, when only moments before there had been dozens of beings milling around. Her muscles coiled, ready to fight if need be, and a hard edge crept into her voice when she asked, "What have you done?"

"I need to speak to you in private, so I have taken us to the Dreams Plain for this conversation."

She blanched. "What in the Four Gods' names do you mean? What's a Dream Plain? Where is everyone?"

"They are here in Ghaia's house still. We are on the Dreams Plain. It is my dream so I can create the space to look however I want."

"Impossible!"

"Difficult. But not impossible for a mythic." The gluxxor croaked out a laugh. "Now stop being hysterical so I can talk. I can't hold us here for long. Tell me, what do you know about this knife?"

She paused, not expecting this line of questioning. "It was my mother's before she died, and my father gifted it to me when I graduated from MINATH. Its name is Firinne. An Alchemist assisted in the forging of the blade, inlaying crystals into the metal to help the knife's owner battle rogue mythics. That's it."

Brother Reikuul's tongue flicked out again and he cocked his head. "One of my gifts is the ability to taste the truth. And what you have said is... not a lie told by you. But there are lies hidden in your statement."

"I'm not lying!"

"Yes, I am aware of that," he said with a bored sigh. "That's what I said. You are not telling the lie, but there is something that tastes wrong about what you know about Firinne. The knife's name is true though, I'll grant you that. But did you realise that you are not using your knife to its full potential?"

"What do you mean?"

He held Firinne up between them. "See these runes on the blade? They've faded because their magic has been depleted. Did you really expect the crystals to work forever?" He snorted in amusement at her ignorance before explaining, "The magic contained within the crystals must be recharged." His tongue flicked out again as he studied her with his milky eyes. Sera shifted uncomfortably under his blind scrutiny, unsure if he could see anything. "It's odd... your aura is fractured. The path you are yet to walk is a twisted one. If you make the right choices, I believe you can aid the mythics of Mandar." He sighed heavily before nodding his scaled head. "I will help you this time."

He uttered strange clicking and croaking sounds in his throat and wove an intricate pattern with his clawed hands. Firinne hovered unsupported in the air between the gluxxor's palms as golden light swirled around the knife before pouring into it. The runes on the blade flashed blinding white. With a low hiss, Brother Reikuul brought his magic to an end and passed Firinne back to Sera.

"How am I supposed to charge it once the magic drains again?" Sera wondered aloud, awestruck by the power she had witnessed. She met the gluxxor's blank stare and asked, "Do I just come back to you?"

Brother Reikuul held up a hand. "We've been here too long. My strength fails me." The Temple flickered in and out of focus in agreement with his declaration. "Good luck, Tracker Seraphina, Goddess knows we will need you in the war to come."

Before Sera could demand more information about this so-called war, she felt a strange sensation of falling before a wave of darkness crashed over her.

CHAPTER THIRTEEN

STIRRING, SERA SLOWLY DRAGGED herself onto her elbows from where she lay on her back. The grass brushed her arms and a stream tinkled beside her. Sitting up, she took stock of her surroundings.

Where am I?

Red bell-headed flowers nodded serenely at her feet and a charming willow tree bowed its head over the running water. Her eyes continued to travel up the tree's trunk until she saw the façade of the Earth Temple behind it. The strange events of her visit to the Dreams Plain came rushing back and she instinctively reached for Firinne. The comforting feel of the staghorn handle met her fingertips and she exhaled in relief. Brother Reikuul had helped her, but something about him set her teeth on edge. Two titters perched on a nearby branch, whispering quietly between themselves and adding the odd indignant chirp through their conversation. They kept looking at her before putting their black beaks back together and muttering. She admired their sleek white feathers and blue breasts, realising she'd never really paid attention to their beauty before.

Normally they're too annoying for me to notice how pretty they are.

They abruptly stopped their chatter and looked her directly in the eye. A shiver passed over her as their beady red eyes held hers, their obvious intelligence striking her. Winging their way towards the ground, both titters swooped low past her ear and chattered, "Save you, need you."

Sera's mouth dropped open, and she called, "Wait! What do you mean?"

The little birds chittered and flitted to the ground in front of her, one hopping forward before the other jumped in front and pecked the other.

"We been sent to you," chirruped one.

"By him," added the other.

"Him? Who's him?" she demanded.

"Not gonna tell you if you rude," squawked the first one.

"We made promise," reprimanded the other. "He eat us, eat us if we don't!"

Sera took a deep breath, praying for patience, and gritted her teeth in what she hoped looked like a smile. "Please. Tell me who sent you, and what they want."

"He want you. Safe. And with him."

"Arius," added the second one. They both nodded in tandem and flitted up and down erratically.

This guy's name keeps popping up. I guess we must have grown close during my time away. A niggle of worry tugged inside her, wondering exactly how close they had gotten and if the feeling was mutual. The fact that she had no memory of him made her doubtful.

At the moment, he's feeling vaguely stalkerish.

She spoke slowly when she addressed the titters next. "Where is he now? Can you take me to him?"

"He coming here. He find you soon," they exclaimed in unison, bobbing their bright heads up and down. Disquiet settled in her stomach and she opened her mouth to ask them more, but they flew away with a screech as they were interrupted by light footsteps on the grass.

"Sera! I was so worried; you disappeared! Why didn't you tell me you were coming outside?" Hazel wrung her hands as she paced in front of Sera, who still sat on the ground where she'd woken.

"I, uh—" She stalled, not quite knowing what to say to Hazel. She decided on a portion of the truth for now. She could share everything with her friend later, once she'd sorted it out in her own mind. "The smell of those moonflowers gave me a headache so I came out here to clear my head. I lost sight of you, sorry, but I was meaning to come back in sooner. I just... got distracted."

Hazel sank to the earth and crossed her legs with a forlorn expression. "I'm sorry, Sera. You're right, Temple isn't your thing. I shouldn't have pushed you to come."

"Don't be daft. It was sweet of you to want to help me. And I'm sure it would have been fine if it wasn't for the headache." She reached out and placed a hand on Hazel's knee. "Please, don't beat yourself up. You're a kind person, and a good friend. I'm lucky to have you."

Hazel's lips trembled and she gave Sera's hand a squeeze before shaking her head and standing up. She reached a hand out, helping Sera to her feet, and said, "It's no more than any friend would do."

Together, they walked out of Ghaia's Garden. As they exited the wrought-iron gates, they ran headfirst into Sera's father.

"I do beg your pardon... girls! Hello! What a surprise to see you here, Sera." Allen raised an eyebrow at his daughter and inclined his head, indicating the Temple behind them.

She eyed her friend and explained drily, "Wasn't my idea."

He chuckled. "Either way, it's good to see you." His eyebrows crumpled and he added in a more serious tone,

"I heard about what happened yesterday. I would have preferred not to hear it from the MRO gossip mill. Why didn't you call me?"

"Sorry, Dad." She hadn't thought to contact her father when she got home, but now he brought it up, she probably should have. "I was exhausted and just wanted to sleep," she said, lamely trying to justify her actions.

He sighed and crossed his arms. "I worry about you, young lady." He pulled her into a hug and added, "I just want you to be safe."

"I know," she murmured, muffled by his shirt.

Allen cleared his throat loudly. "Well, if you're feeling up to it, how about we go for a hike out to Del's tomorrow? She sent a message asking you to visit."

"That's a good idea, Sera," Hazel added. "It might get your mind off your worries."

Allen smiled pleasantly at Hazel before continuing, "I was as surprised as you to learn she was your grandmother." He shook his head. "That still blows my mind. I can't believe she only told us now, after all these years of going to see her. And your mother never mentioned a thing..." He coughed briefly before knitting his brow. "In fact, she told me all of her family were gone. That's why I took your mother's last name when we married. I didn't want her to feel so alone in the world. It's strange that neither of them ever told us the truth, but I'm sure they had their reasons." He coughed again, louder this time, and wiped a hand over his forehead. "I might head home, for now. I'm suddenly feeling quite unwell."

Headache forgotten, Sera tilted her head apprehensively. "What's wrong, Dad? How can I help?"

"I'd say I got a little too much sun this week. Don't you worry yourself about me, I'll be fine." With that he bent over and commenced a coughing fit that shook his entire body. Hazel and Sera shared a look of alarm.

"Dad!"

He waved a hand at her, dismissing her concern. "I'm fine," he wheezed.

"You don't sound it," Sera insisted.

At that point Hazel stepped forward. "Come on, Mr Azura. How about you go home to rest now and I'll meet you there once I've grabbed a tincture for that cough from my supply. That should do the trick. Don't worry about a thing, Sera, I'll get him fixed up in no time. You can relax for the rest of the day and I'll see you tonight."

Sera folded her arms. "I'm not leaving him like this. I'm coming with you."

"Sera," Hazel murmured, her tone gentle. "I know you want to look after your dad, but you can't do that if you don't look after yourself, too. You've had a crazy few weeks. Between your injuries and your mental health, you're on the verge of burning out. Go home and rest. I've got the medicine to help Allen's cough. He'll be fine with me."

Worrying her lip, Sera studied her father.

Allen straightened, his breathing coming a little easier, and squeezed her arm reassuringly. "I'll be fine, Sera. Hazel will sort me out. I'll call you tomorrow and let you know if I'm well enough to join you on the hike to Del's." His lips lifted at the indecision painted plainly on her face and added, "I'll let you know if I get any worse, okay?"

Sera opened her mouth to argue further, but Hazel interrupted. "He won't get better any faster if he's worrying about you too."

Blowing out an exasperated breath, Sera begrudgingly conceded. "Fine. But make sure you call me if anything changes, all right?" She hugged her father fiercely.

Allen smiled into her hair. "I promise."

CHAPTER FOURTEEN

TAKING THE LONG WAY back to her apartment Sera wandered along the streets of Mandar City, relishing the sights and smells of the bustling capital. The fear that constricted her heart over her father's abrupt illness eased slightly as she drifted down the empty pavement. The aroma that wafted her way from the various cafes captivated her senses, so she stopped to buy a coffee and a boysenberry scroll. She walked aimlessly as she snacked, with no set path in mind, flakes of pastry dropping onto her shirt, until she found herself standing in front of Alistair's shop. It was a mess.

She stared numbly at the boarded-up windows and broken glass, her mind not willing to process the truth in front of her. Peering through a crack, she searched the interior for any sign of the gargoyle. The store was completely empty. All the carvings had been removed and there was no indication that her friend had been there for quite some time. She tried to count back how long it had been since she'd last visited him.

Was it three weeks? Or four? What happened to him?

Turning the handle, she pushed against the door but it wouldn't budge. She ran a hand over her face, concern for her friend running rampant, and wondered who she could ask who might have heard what happened. She pulled her phone out and tapped the screen, finger hovering over it as she contemplated who to contact. After a moment of deliberation, she decided to message her father.

'Hey Dad, are you home now? Has Hazel got her medicine for you yet? I hope you're feeling a little better. I was just wondering whether you know what happened to Alistair's shop? I've just walked past and it's all boarded up. Love you xo'

She stood there staring at the mess, wondering where Alistair was and what had happened. A small, horrible voice whispered in her mind that maybe his dragon carving had been found and he'd been thrown in the IRC. She shook her head to dispel the thought and marched over to a nearby bin, throwing her paper bag and coffee cup in before returning to the store front. She tapped her foot anxiously against the pavement while she waited for a reply. Her phone vibrated with her father's response.

'Sorry, I forgot to tell you. Apparently, he's moved away and the shop is up for lease now. I'm home now and Hazel won't be far away. Stop worrying. Love you X'

Her heart twisted and her lips pulled down. She hadn't even had a chance to say goodbye to her stony friend. Looking again at the mess, concern bubbled up in her chest. Alistair would never leave the property in this state. She tapped her thumbs quickly over the phone once more.

'Good, I'm glad you're home safe. Thanks, I wondered why it was empty. It's strange that it's been left in such a mess. I would have thought Alistair would leave it in perfect condition?'

This time she didn't have to wait long for a reply.

'That is strange. Perhaps some vandals have been into it. Might be worth reporting. But go home and rest first. You had a big day yesterday. Love you, sweetheart X'

'Will do. Love you too Dad. Feel better xo'

Knowing the Department of Property and Leasing preferred online reports as opposed to phone calls, Sera lodged a report for vandalism on the website for DOPL. She automatically tucked her phone into her back pocket but paused when it hit something solid. Blanking for a moment she suddenly remembered the Seeing Stone. Shoving her phone into the opposite pocket, she pulled out the Seeing Stone and, on a whim, closed her eyes and held the image of Alistair in her mind. Opening her eyes, she watched as the surface darkened and a building appeared. Behind the structure, clouds scudded across the night sky, making it difficult to pick out details. Peering closely, she noticed the stuffed raven on the front gate and realised with a start that it was her nanna's cottage. Glancing between the Seeing Stone and Alistair's shop, she contemplated whether there was a connection between the two or if it was just a random vision. Once the image faded, she placed the Stone safely back in her pocket and walked away from the shop.

As she reached the intersection where she would normally turn left to return to her apartment, a prickle of unease made the hair stand up on her arms. Glancing behind her, she didn't see anyone but had a feeling she was being followed. She paused only for a moment, then crossed the road and continued straight without looking back again. If she was right, Sera didn't want to lead the stranger to her home. It would be best to confront whoever they were in a public place. Thinking quickly, she considered her options. The closest densely populated place would be the library. Taking a moment to plan her route, she slunk against the doorway of a closed clothes store. Her heart thumped loudly as she scanned the road behind her. There was no one there. Her shoulders slumped as she took a shuddering breath and tried to calm the adrenaline racing through her body.

Maybe I'm just being paranoid. It has been a stressful couple of days. Now I'm just making up stalkers.

She had almost decided to walk back to her home when a shadowy figure flitted between a concrete wall and an electronic noticeboard. Narrowing her eyes, Sera hissed softly as her adrenaline kicked back into overdrive. She was right. Someone was tailing her.

Spinning to her right, she sped down the pavement. The close of the work day meant that the number of pedestrians had increased, so she forced herself to be careful to avoid running into any other mythics or humans in her rush. Casting a quick peek over her shoulder, she saw the mysterious person again. A brief study of the figure made her almost certain he was a male, and she wondered why he'd been following her. She increased her pace into almost a sprint and internally sighed with relief when she saw the grand vision of the city library. The building was made mainly of glass and stainless steel, an imposing piece of architecture. There were no bookstores in Mandar City, but the library more than made up for it.

Her footsteps pounded against the concrete steps as she raced up to the front entrance. Shoving against the glass revolving door, she willed it to move faster. After what seemed like an age, but was really no more than a few seconds, she burst onto the library's main floor. There were two levels in the library, each with thousands of books lining the shelves. There were a few people seated around the study tables and a couple of mythics curled up on the lounges, reading quietly. Sera cursed inwardly. She had anticipated more of a crowd.

It will be okay. This is better than being caught alone in the elevator of my apartment.

Turning around, she faced the front door defiantly, waiting for her pursuer to show himself. A gaggle of MI-NATH apprentices pushed through the revolving door, chatting and giggling amongst themselves as they advanced towards the desks. They gave her a strange look as they walked past, probably wondering why she glared at the doors so darkly. Shortly after, a man entered. Sera couldn't help but gasp as he strode towards her. His coffee-coloured hair hung loose past his bare shoulders where an old scar traced his collarbone. Another scar, golden in colour and similar to hers, ran over the left side of his chest. Sera tore her eyes away from his body where muscles rippled beneath the lean frame, hinting at danger in the way they coiled, ready for battle. His shirtless state earned a few more giggles from the nearby students. The librarian glowered at the noise and they buried their noses in textbooks, occasionally peeking over the top to look at the half-naked man. Sera considered asking for their help but ruled against it.

For now.

She stared into his eyes, where the green irises swirled, and yelped as a searing heat ripped through her left hand. Glancing down, she saw the thin golden scar on her palm shining faintly. She balled her hand into a fist and scowled at the stranger. She didn't understand why, but she had a feeling he was the reason she was reacting this way. Her body tensed, ready to run if necessary, and she waited for him to approach.

"Seraphina!" The man's voice was hoarse with desperation, and something that sounded like longing.

"How do you know my name?" She stepped back, her right hand tensed, ready to unsheathe Firinne if necessary.

"You... you don't remember me?" His face fell. "That's impossible. We're Soulbound." He moved closer and captured a strand of auburn hair that had escaped her ponytail, tucking it tenderly behind her ear.

She jerked back and glared at him, enraged by his familiarity. "Don't presume to touch me, sir. And what in the Four Gods' names is Soulbound? Whatever it is, I'm pretty sure we're not, considering I don't know you." She took a few more steps back and bumped into a bookshelf. He kept following her, his searing gaze never leaving hers. Her heart jumped in her chest at the yearning in his expression and her heavy breathing sounded too loud to her ears. He reached for her again, so she blindly grabbed a book from behind her and threw it at him. It smacked him in the face and dropped to the floor in a heap. The man blinked at her, shock coating his features. It would have almost looked comical had she not been so afraid and confused by his claims.

"Show me your hand," he commanded, with a sudden expression of passion. Glowering obstinately, she raised her right hand to face him.

With a snort of amusement at her deliberate attempt to misguide him, he said, "No, show me the palm of your left hand."

Narrowing her eyes, she hesitantly brought her left hand up, the golden scar facing him. He mirrored her action to show his own scar. She sucked in a breath in shock.

"Where did you get that?" she demanded.

Sadness stained his features and he said, "You must have been touched by a dark magic to have forgotten me so completely. That explains why you ran." He offered a melancholy smile and said, "It is me, Arius."

She stared, nonplussed. "I'm sorry," she offered. "I met Tor and Idris who told me your name, but I don't remember you. I have no memory of anything that happened between shooting the doe and waking up on the road near Grave's Point."

"Nothing?" he asked huskily as he rubbed the matching gold mark on his chest.

She shook her head. His eyes roamed over her face, tracing lines of heat as they continued to travel over her body. She blushed at his intensity and wondered again at their previous friendship. His gaze darkened as her cheeks bloomed and he stepped forward, grabbing her hair roughly with one hand whilst the other circled her waist, and crushed his lips to hers. Disbelief froze her in place for a moment as electricity thrilled through her body. His lips moved against hers, setting her nerves on fire, until she managed to gather her frayed thoughts back into coherency. She pulled her right arm free of his hold and punched him in the face.

CHAPTER FIFTEEN

SERA GATHERED SOME ICE cubes from the freezer in her apartment and poured them into a tea towel. Walking over to the couch, she handed the homemade ice pack to Arius and crossed her arms, standing over the man.

"I'm not apologising. I don't care what our history might be, if a woman says she doesn't remember you, you don't just go and kiss her."

He pressed the ice pack to his cheek and grinned. "To be fair, I thought it might help jog your memory. And, if I'm honest, your reaction has made me love you even more. Which I didn't think was possible..." he trailed off as he glanced at the darkening sky out her window.

"Four Gods help us! There you go again! Love? Love! I don't know you! Maybe I did, but even then, I was gone for less than a fortnight. That's not enough time to fall in love with someone. You can't come in here spouting your declarations of love for me!"

He flashed another charming smile. "You are right, of course. I apologise. Please forgive my forwardness. I'll be on my best behaviour from now on."

"If you do it again, I'm throwing you out," Sera grumbled. A sudden embarrassing thought had her pinching the bridge of her nose. "Arius... when we... met previously... did we...?" She groaned, unable to finish the sentence.

He chuckled. "No. We did not make love. Even with all your memories intact you were strong enough to deny me."

She cringed at the term, but was thankful they didn't have a physical past that she'd forgotten. As she watched him adjust his position on the couch to get more comfortable, her eyes lingered on the bare skin of his shoulders and trailed down the planes of his chest. Heat pooled in her core and she tore her eyes away and cleared her throat self-consciously. Grabbing them both a glass of water, she spun a dining chair around to face the lounge and sat down, the coffee table acting as a barrier between them. She opened her mouth to interrogate him but was interrupted by a loud meow. Perry stalked up to Arius, tail erect and fur raised. Sera waited for the inevitable attack as the tomcat studied the strange man. Her jaw dropped when the tabby purred and rubbed his cheek against Arius's leg before rolling onto his back playfully.

"Who is this delightful creature?" asked Arius as he scratched under Perry's chin.

Delightful is not an adjective I would have used to describe that cat.

As Sera awkwardly watched the strange exchange, she was saved from answering by the opening of the front door. Hazel entered the apartment, chattering away about the upcoming Choosing Ceremony, but stopped short when she noticed their visitor.

"Oh, hi there! Sorry, I didn't realise we were expecting company." She shot Sera a questioning look as she walked around to the front of the couch and pasted a smile on her lips. "I'm Hazel." She held her hand out but yelped in surprise when Arius ceased scratching Perry's chin to meet her handshake.

He looked between the two women, hand hanging in the air, confusion marking his forehead with a crease. "I don't understand what's happening. I thought this was an accepted form of greeting?"

Hazel giggled and explained, "Perry is my cat and he hates everyone. Especially strangers. The fact that he's warmed to you immediately is... surprising to say the least."

"I see. Thank you for explaining, Hazel. I am Arius. I am Seraphina's Soulbound."

"Her what now?" Hazel looked at Sera, bewildered.

Sera shrugged helplessly at Hazel before turning her grimace to Arius. "You're doing that overfamiliar thing again," she remonstrated.

He ducked his head with a chuckle and held his hands up in surrender. "Sorry. I'll stop."

She snorted. "I don't think you can, but at least the thought is there." She gestured to the lanky man taking up most of the space on their couch. "This is Arius. Apparently, we met during my time away. I don't remember him, but we have matching scars on our chest and palm, and he claims to be my Soulbound." She shrugged before Hazel could ask. "No, I don't know what that is, and I'm not sure I want to."

"Ri-ight." The way her friend dragged out the word made it sound like two syllables rather than one. Hazel shook her head in astonishment. "That's a lot to take in. I'm sure there's plenty more to the story too. Would you care to stay for dinner, Arius? We can chat about it. Maybe you can help Sera piece back together what happened on her trip?"

Arius said, "I'm sorry, but I have to take my leave. While I can maintain this form longer while I am near you, I am growing weak and can only regain my strength by returning to my true form."

"Your what?" Sera asked, puzzled.

His mouth twisted sadly and he said, "Of course, you won't remember that. I can't explain now, but I will tomorrow once I have recovered."

Realisation dawned and Sera asked, "Are you a type of shifter?"

A beat passed before Arius replied with a soft smile, "Of sorts. But whatever you do, don't let my father hear you call me that. He would consider it the gravest of insults to be compared to one he considers a lower mythic."

Sera's eyes widened but she didn't comment on his father's judgemental views. "I have plans tomorrow morning, but maybe we could meet up tomorrow night? You might be allowed to stay for dinner, if you can behave yourself."

He acquiesced, before standing in one smooth motion and taking a few fluid strides to her side. Sera sucked in a tiny gasp at his sudden proximity as he loomed over her, staring deep into her soul. She couldn't deny the connection she felt to him, even if she couldn't remember him from before. He passed the ice pack back to her with a murmured thanks and leant down to peck her on the cheek. Then he left. With his departure Sera felt a tug in her chest and the scar on her palm flared in pain. Shaking her head, she pushed against the powerful emotions that rose unbidden. Standing up abruptly, she stalked to the lounge room window and looked out into the sky, crossing her arms.

Hazel gave a low whistle and joined her at the window. "So... he's cute. Do you like him?"

"Honestly, I'm... undecided. It's so hard without knowing what happened between us before. He seems nice and

I feel... attached to him, but that doesn't guarantee that he's not playing me for a fool. What if he kidnapped me or something and has come back to take me away?"

"Good point. Don't let down your guard with him."

"I don't intend to." Shaking her head, Sera tried to dispel the distracting thoughts of the strange man who had unexpectedly burst into her life that afternoon. Turning to Hazel, she asked, "How was Dad when you left him?"

Hazel placed a reassuring hand on her arm. "Allen will be fine, Sera. I gave him Cough Cure and Deep Sleep. He'll get a solid night's rest while the Cough Cure does its work."

"Thank you so much for taking care of him, Hazel."

"I'm happy to help. Come on, stop worrying and come have some dinner."

"I'm not hungry." Sera offered a soft smile and added, "I'm just really tired. Think I'll go to bed early."

Her friend gave her a searching look then stepped back. "Of course. I can only imagine. Get some rest, but please tell me if you need anything."

Sera nodded and gave her friend a tight hug. When Sera pulled away, she noticed a rosy blush warming Hazel's cheeks. Amused by her apparent embarrassment from her display of affection, Sera put some distance between them and said, "I'm glad I've got you."

Even after a hot shower and lying quietly in bed for an hour, Sera's stomach was still tying itself in knots. There was no way she could have kept dinner down even if she had been hungry. Anxiety ate away at her as she replayed the events of the last two days. So much had happened, yet all it had done was raise more questions. The worry about Balthazar's recovery and the unexpected illness of her father threatened her rationality and she stamped down a pang of unease. The horrifying loss of the Unicorn King still weighed on her conscience and the strange meeting of the harpy, Tor and Idris baffled her. Then there was Arius. There was no denying the feelings he stirred in her, but she couldn't decide whether to trust him. Perhaps he was the reason she'd lost her memories. Tossing in bed, she closed her eyes and tried reciting a chant the medical team had recommended to help her sleep. Thankful she didn't have an audience for her average singing voice, she closed her eyes and kept her breathing even through the nonsense words they'd taught her.

"Sah, nah, tah, kah." The refrain echoed in the room until she drifted off to sleep. Images jumped through her mind's eye as she dreamed of a faceless harpy that stalked her as she cried over Balthazar who lay disembowelled in the middle of the MRO. The dream shifted to her sobbing over her father's grave as a titter pecked her ears until they bled. She sensed a comforting warmth at her back so she turned and ran towards the golden light. The air shifted and shimmered around her and turned to night. She soared through the air, high above Mandar City, watching the tiny pinpricks of light in the high-rises wink out as their occupants succumbed to slumber. The air flowed easily beneath her leathery wings as they caught a current and rose higher. Intuitively, she sensed she had to stay out of sight of any being who happened to look towards the stars. The feeling of freedom was indescribable as she winged between the clouds, feeling the currents of the air and admiring the city laid out below her.

Seraphina? The warm male voice in her head shocked her.

Who is that? Why are you in my head? Sera swung her head left and right, seeking out the intruder.

A soft chuckle answered her. *It's Arius. And as a matter of fact, it is you who is in my head. Although, with no memories of our time together, I didn't think you would still be able to make the connection.*

She paused as she mulled over his words then gave her head a shake. *This is a strange dream.*

It's no dream. His tone was warm but firm. *You have an extraordinary power that allows you entry into my mind. And the mind of other dragons.*

She snorted. *Yeah, right. That's how I know this is a dream. Dragons are extinct.*

Arius' voice turned melancholy. *We need to find a way for you to get your memories back.*

You think I don't know that?

Arius tried another angle. *Look around you. What do you see? What do you feel? What do you hear?*

Sera slowed her flight and took stock of her surroundings. The wispy clouds scudded across the dark sky, filtering the moonlight on her scaled body. She flexed her sharp talons and admired the coppery scales adorning her muscular form. She arched her long neck and felt the wind ripple through the spikes lining her spine. The cold light of the stars prickled the sensitive membrane of her massive wings. Sweet voices sang softly in a strange language. Swinging her head around, she scanned the skies for the owners.

Where is that song coming from?

That is Illundar.

A thread of a memory tickled her thoughts. *I know that word.*

We've had this conversation before, he confirmed.

She grasped the memory tightly before it could slip away. *It means... starsong.*

Yes! Do you remember? He sounded ecstatic.

Nothing else. Only the meaning of that word. So, what, the stars are singing?

Yes. You've flown with me and heard them before.

That's... unbelievable. She said the word reverently but meant it in its literal sense as well. Fatigue pulled her mind away from the connection but she heard Arius one last time.

Rest now, Seraphina. I will watch over you tonight.

She returned to her own thoughts, slipping into a deep and restful sleep, cocooned in the warmth of Arius' protection.

CHAPTER SIXTEEN

THE NEXT DAY DAWNED bright and Sera bounced out of bed, feeling more rested than she had since she'd returned to the city. Stretching, she felt her joints pop as she took a few deep breaths, unable to contain the smile that played over her lips. The sense of freedom and safety in her dream about flying through the sky as a dragon spilled over into the real-world, injecting positivity into her mood.

I don't care if it was only a dream. It's nice to feel genuinely happy for a change.

Checking her phone she saw two texts: one from Hazel and one from her father. Her friend's message was simply wishing Sera a good day, while her father's explained that he was still too sick to join her on her visit to Del. One of her dreams from last night resurfaced in her mind's eye; the image of the gravestone with her father's name on it dampening her sunny disposition. She forced herself to ignore the prickle of worry and firmly reprimanded her wayward imagination.

People get sick all the time. There's no reason why Dad won't fully recover. I'm stressing about nothing.

Regardless of her internal assurances, she called her father to put her concern to rest. "Hey Dad, how're you going?" Even after almost convincing herself he was fine, Sera's apprehension was obvious.

"I'm all right, sweetheart." Allen tone was cheery but his voice grated.

Her brows kissed and she pressed for details. "You mentioned in your text that you weren't well enough to hike today. Are you sure you're okay? I can cancel my visit to Del and come over, if you'd like?"

"No, no! Don't change your plans," he insisted. A cough disrupted his next sentence. "Hazel sent some chicken broth over and she left more of her medicine. I'll be doing nothing all day; just resting. It will be very boring. Go visit Del and tell her I said, hello."

"Are you sure, Dad? It's no trouble. I don't mind doing nothing all day if it helps you feel better."

"It will make me feel better to know my daughter is spending an enjoyable day with her grandmother, not stuck in a dark room trying to avoid waking her dad. Go. It will be good for you." He stifled a yawn.

"Okay, okay, I'll go. Rest up. I'll talk later. Love you, Dad."

"Love you too, sweetheart. Have fun. Bye."

She smiled as he hung up, thankful he didn't seem worse. Sending a brief reply to Hazel, she followed it with a quick text to her grandmother to say she was on her way to visit. Sera had convinced Del to get a mobile phone after she'd found out about their relationship so they could stay in touch. It was a lot easier than trekking out there every time she wanted to speak to her. She swiftly tied her tresses back in a braid and, before leaving her bedroom, stopped for a moment and looked at herself in the mirror. The dark circles that had taken up permanent residence under her eyes lately had lightened, her skin looked clearer and her sapphire-blue eyes shone brightly. Wisps of auburn hair had already escaped the braid and curled charmingly around her cheeks. She flashed a smile at her reflection, thankful for the overwhelming sense of contentment after a dreary week.

She took the time to cook herself bacon and eggs on toast and brewed a small pot of coffee, whistling cheerily as she moved around the kitchen, and tossed a rasher to Perry, much to his surprise. She threw the dirty dishes in the dishwasher and turned it on before returning to her room to get dressed. Considering her measly supply of outfits, she shrugged and grabbed her usual black trousers and green shirt. Even on her days off, she tended to wear her Tracker uniform. After a moment's hesitation, she grabbed her leather jacket. Whilst the sun was shining today the season was changing, and a slight chill pervaded the air.

Before leaving her room, she made sure the necklace that Helena had given her was tucked safely against her chest and the Seeing Stone was snug in her pocket. Threading Firinne's sheath to her belt, she grabbed her new backpack and threw a canteen of water in along with her MRO Survival Kit. From force of habit, after shutting the front door she waited a moment until she heard the locks automatically click. Running for the elevator, she managed to slip in before the doors closed. A gluxxor met her gaze and nodded once before turning away to stare vacantly at the wood-panelled walls of the lift. Unease stole over Sera as she recalled the interaction with the gluxxor from Ghaia's Temple. Somehow, he'd stolen her into the Dreams Plain and raised so many questions without offering any explanations. She shivered, but strove to banish her apprehension. This gluxxor was female and had a kind expression. She was no threat. Still, Sera couldn't help but rush through the doors as soon as they slid open onto the foyer.

Jogging down the road, she ducked into the grocers and bought some supplies for Del. The old woman grew a lot of vegetables and herbs in her garden and trapped animals for meat, but that didn't mean she didn't have a use for flour, sugar and canned goods. With her backpack now bulging, Sera began her trek south-west towards the path in the forest that would lead her to her nanna's cottage.

The day heated up as Sera walked beside a creek and she stopped to remove her jacket. It took some shuffling, but she managed to shove it inside the backpack, on top of the groceries. Sweat dripped down her neck and she swiped it away grumpily.

Where has my nice, cool autumn day gone?

She was only a few minutes from Del's now, so at least she would find some reprieve from the humidity shortly. Dark clouds appeared out of nowhere and obscured the late morning sunlight. An unnatural mist rolled in, snaking through the trees and putting Sera on edge. It had been too warm a day for there to be any mist and this grew thicker by the minute. She shivered as the temperature plummeted abruptly and stopped to pull out her jacket from her backpack. Squinting as she drew closer to her grandmother's house, she pushed open the gate, ignoring the creepy stuffed raven, and made her way up the path towards the crooked log cabin.

"Hi, Del!" Silence met her greeting. "Oops, I should call you Nanna, right? That's going to take some getting used to." She frowned and scanned the garden for the wizened old woman. The shrubs were more overgrown than usual and there was no sign of movement within the house.

Something's wrong.

Tracker instincts humming, she dropped the heavy backpack from her shoulders and tucked it against the rickety fence. Keeping to the perimeter of the yard she slunk through the garden as she pulled Firinne out. She sniffed the air and turned her head, utilising all her senses in the hopes it would lead to a clue of her grandmother's whereabouts. Something felt amiss, and the atmosphere was heavy with the threat of an impending electrical storm. After circling the house without incident, she stood back at the gate, undecided on her next action.

"That's weird," she muttered as she stared at the stuffed raven on the gate. She could have sworn its head was turned towards the forest last time she was here. Now it stared at the house. As she watched, it blinked. She clapped a hand over her mouth, smothering her squeal as she leapt back.

A hoarse voice croaked from the raven, "Come closer."

Heart thumping, Sera glanced around again before taking a tentative step towards what she had thought until now was just a stuffed bird. The eyes of the raven watched her impatiently, though the rest of its body remained frozen.

Unsure of what it wanted, she allowed her instincts to take over and raised a hand to softly pet the feathers around its head. As soon as her hand touched it, the black bird lunged and struck her wrist, drawing blood. She squealed aloud this time and clutched her hand to her chest. The raven threw its head back and drank her blood that had smeared over its beak.

"That's better," he cawed, stretching his wings and fluffing his feathers.

"What in Ghaia's name are you? And why did you bite me?" Sera glared accusingly at the mythic, no doubt in her mind now that that was what it was. Precisely what species of mythic was another question.

"Titchy, aren't we," he guffawed. "Here, here, allow me to attend your wound. I can fix it."

"I don't trust you not to do it again, you bloodthirsty wretch."

He cawed a few times in mirth and hopped along the gate, closer to her. "Fair enough, fair enough. Here, I'll make you a deal. Give me your hand to mend, and then I'll take you to your grandmother."

"How do you know she's—"

"Your grandmother? Del tells me everything. Everything." He hung his beak open in a strange smile. "We'll explain it all soon, but I really do need to heal your wound so your blood doesn't attract any... undesirables."

Eying him distrustfully, Sera held her hand out hesitantly. The raven leant down and examined the cut that still seeped blood. He turned his head sharply, plucked a feather from his wing and held the quill in his beak. A bead of oil slid down the feather and dropped onto her wrist. She gasped as it sizzled on her skin and the cut knit itself back together. Amazed, she wiped the blood away and inspected the fresh skin.

"That's incredible!"

"Yes, yes, I know, I tell Del all the time that she severely underappreciates my talents, but does she listen?" He rolled his eyes melodramatically. "By the way, I'm Fray. It's a pleasure to formally meet you, Seraphina. But we must fly now." With a squawk he flew swiftly to the tree line and perched on the low-hanging branch of a rowan tree. "Come quick, come quick."

She dashed after him but skidded to a stop when he flew to her shoulder, dug his claws in and hissed, "Quietly, silly girl!"

"Ow! You told me to come quickly!"

"Be quick *and* quiet." The bird scowled at her before glancing skyward. "We are being watched."

"By whom?"

"I'm not sure. I only know it is a powerful soul who hides in those clouds. We must hide and run." He nodded vehemently. "Hide and run." He released her shoulder and darted into the foliage.

"Where are we going?" she whispered.

"Can't say, can't say. He might hear," came the soft response, hidden among the leaves.

Sera stopped under the cover of the rowan tree and peered through the greenery, trying to find Fray through the fog. The sigh of a wingbeat brushed her cheek and she bit back a squeak of surprise before hurrying after the black bird. Pushing through the dense shrubs that had claimed the forest floor, she hissed as thorns dug into her legs, even through her trousers. The strange mist permeated the air and wound itself around her waist. Grimacing, she glanced down to see the silvery tendrils thickening around her and slowing her momentum.

"Fray!" she called as loudly as she dared. "We've got a problem."

He returned to her side and screeched in distress. He flapped his wings violently in an attempt to disperse the mist. While it swept some of it aside, the remainder solidified into a tangible rope coiled around her body.

"This is not how I die," she growled into the empty air, aiming her anger at whoever had spelled the mist. Twisting and jerking, she leant forward, fighting against its pull. The more she battled, the stronger it grew, until eventually she was forced to a standstill. She continued to struggle, refusing to give up.

Fray perched on a branch in front of her and cawed once before his eyes rolled into the back of his head. A pair of blue human eyes now looked out from his. Fray's beak fell open and he spoke with Del's voice, "Use Firinne. Then run as fast as you can."

The fear in her grandmother's voice sent cold shivers through Sera. Fray's usual beady black eyes returned and he gave his feathers a shake.

Sera shut her mouth with a snap. *Time to focus now. You can process the fact that Del can take control of animals later.*

Unsure of how effective her blade would be against the mist, she hesitated. When she started getting dragged back the way she had come, she decided to trust Del's instructions and swept her knife through the sparkling strands. It would be beautiful if it wasn't so frightening. As she cut the ethereal rope, she realised the runes on the blade were glowing faintly. Each slice of Firinne loosened the hold the mist had around her waist until eventually, the last thread fell. Sera sprang away and Fray flew in front of her, guiding her. She crashed blindly through the thicket, ignoring the pain as she focused on following the raven over the uneven ground. A guttural bellow of fury echoed around the valley and sent a spike of adrenaline stampeding through her body. Her feet pounded into the earth as she ran. Leaping over fallen logs, pushing through vines and scraping her hands against the bark as she bounced off trees in the dim light, Sera pushed her body to the limit as she sensed the great beast in the sky gaining on them.

"Into the cave, into the cave," cawed Fray frantically.

Without a second thought of what might be waiting for her in the complete darkness, she hurdled through the entry just as a ball of fire hit the earth where she had been only moments before. Slipping on loose stones, she ran, unseeing, into the belly of the cave. The ground unexpectedly fell away from beneath her and she felt herself falling. Arms flailing and eyes wide, she desperately sought something to grab onto to slow her descent. With no light to see the rocky walls flying past her, it was a shock when the lung-crushing force smacked into her as her body hit the ground.

CHAPTER SEVENTEEN

SERA GROANED. SHE TRIED to suck in a deep breath, but the wind had been knocked out of her. She tamped down the rising panic, knowing her breathing would return to normal soon – she simply had to relax and breathe deeply. Focusing on making her stomach rise, she pulled in another breath. Keeping her eyes tightly shut, she wiggled her toes and fingers to see if anything vital had broken in her freefall. When they responded as normal, she relaxed a little. Fray cawed loudly in the darkness, forcing Sera to open her eyes. She couldn't make out anything in the void that surrounded her. Twisting her hand around, she felt the handle of Firinne and grasped it tightly.

Lucky I didn't land on that.

"Fray?" she wheezed as she forcibly drew another breath into her lungs and struggled to her feet.

"I'm here," he replied and she felt his comforting weight land on her shoulder. He leaned his head against her cheek and crooned, "Are you all right? All right?"

"I will be." She turned her head, eyes scanning the dark, but remained blind. She asked the bird, "Can you see anything?"

"Yes, yes, yes. We have company."

"What? Why didn't you say so earlier?" she cried and dropped into a fighting stance, raising Firinne to defend her front, even though she had no idea which side an attack would be coming from.

"Because I am a friend," rumbled a gravelly voice from the darkness.

Sera's eyebrows kissed and she lowered her weapon at the familiar tone. "Is that you, Alistair?"

A chuckle met her, then a flash of light blurred her vision as an LED torch was turned on. "Good to see you, Seraphina."

"Oh, Alistair!" She flung herself at the tall gargoyle and hugged his mid-section, ignoring the uncomfortable sensation of cuddling cold stone. "It's so good to see you, too! I was really worried when I saw your shop all boarded up!"

"I had to disappear for a while."

She pulled back and frowned at him. "What do you mean?"

He waved his hand in the air, dismissing her question. "That's not important right now. There's something I need to ask you."

"And what would that be?" She cocked an eyebrow.

"What happened to you during your time away?"

She cast her arms wide and said, "I don't know! I've lost all my memories from the first day of my trip until a week and a half later when I woke up on the road to Grave's Point."

He nodded solemnly. "I had heard that much on the grapevine while I was in hiding, but hoped my source was wrong." He strode over to his pack and rummaged inside for a time. Sera took the moment to study the cavern in the torchlight. Looking up, she could see the tunnel through which she'd fallen after her headlong flight into the unknown depths of the cave. Explosions echoed from the tunnel overhead, but Sera wasn't sure if they came from the thunderstorm or the creature that hunted her. Dropping her eyes, she tracked Alistair's movements and saw only his pack and a small collection of belongings strewn around the cave. It was strange to see him without the company of his carved creations. Another explosion rocked the earth above and a shower of dirt scuttled down the cave walls.

"What is that out there?"

Alistair froze for a beat, then turned to her with a grave expression and something small hidden in his large grey hands. "It's a dragon."

"Don't be ridiculous. They're extinct."

Strange how last night I dreamt about being a dragon and today I'm being chased by what Alistair claims is one. I don't usually believe in coincidences. This is... odd, at the very least. But it doesn't change the fact that dragons died out in the Mythic War.

The fireball that had exploded from the sky and nearly stolen her life rose to the surface of her mind. That was hard to explain away.

Could they have survived without us knowing?

Doubt shadowed her thoughts as she considered the possibility. Sera shook her head vehemently, denying the potential existence of any other reality. The government would have found out about any dragons that survived and sent Trackers and Hunters after them. The dragons were gone. When she met the gaze of her gargoyle friend again, he stepped towards her and revealed the sculpture he cradled so carefully. It was the tiny dragon he had carved for her over a month ago.

He held it out and said, "I have my own theories about what happened while you were gone. But this carving will reveal the truth to you."

"Wait, what? Are you saying that this dragon statue will somehow magically bring my memories back?" She eyed him sceptically.

He nodded silently and thrust it closer. She instinctively cringed back from the forbidden mythic but, with gritted teeth, forced herself to stretch her hand towards it. Clasping it firmly around the body, she brought it up to her eyes. Once again, she admired the detail of each scale, tooth and claw. Somehow, Alistair had managed to make the wings appear almost translucent. The sapphire eyes captured and held her attention. The blue stones shimmered in the bright light of the torch with something bordering on sentience. Warmth radiated from the core of the statue and it began to glow, softly at first, until the blue light solidified into a bright aura around the carving.

The tiny stone dragon came to life in her palm and flapped its wings before weaving tenderly around her arm. It climbed onto her shoulders, curling around her neck briefly in a loving embrace before descending down her other arm to her bruised elbow. Lines of light coiled around her body in the wake of the tiny dragon's path, but unlike the mist from earlier, it offered a wonderful sense of comfort. Sera couldn't help but grin at the animated statue. It shot her an apologetic smile before returning its attention to the blue-green patch of skin in the crook of her elbow, opened its mouth and struck.

Sera cried out as her skin was torn open and blood poured from the gaping wound. Before she could fling her attacker away, the blue glow that still poured from the dragon's body plunged into her arm through the site of the injury. Her body involuntarily stiffened as beams pulsed through her veins, cleansing the darkness that had dogged her steps ever since she'd woken up on the road into Mandar City without her memories. Everything came flooding back as the poison the President had injected her with was flushed out.

The awe of the first night when she had joined minds with her dragon.

The wondering whether he would devour her before she could escape.

The anxiety when Arius met with the other dragons to discuss her future.

The relief when he'd returned in time to save her from the night scamps.

The joy of soaring through the sky with him.

The love she felt for him, even before they bound their souls together.

Memories flashed through her mind as she recalled meeting Tor, Idris, Aliah, Desamor, Talegar and the harpy. The night when she and Arius crashed from the sky and were separated at the lake hit her like a physical blow. Her knees buckled and she dropped to the ground as all the events that had led her to this moment overwhelmed her senses. It left her gasping for air as she tried to assimilate her new truth. She stopped resisting and allowed the onslaught of memories to wash over her, leaning into them as they consumed her like fire. They raced through her mind over and over as the truth sank into her skin. She shook and retched, the power of her story sinking deep into her soul and expelling the mental barrier that had haunted her for too long. Eyes as wide as the moon, Sera's jaw hung open as she returned to herself. She stared at Alistair.

"I remember," she whispered. "I remember... everything."

Alistair nodded sagely. "Good. Your aura has shifted and the block has lifted."

Lurching back to her feet, she leant down and collected the carving of the dragon from where it lay. It had returned to its original state, though its sapphire eyes had dulled.

Rubbing her arms, she took a shaking breath. "Alistair... the dragons aren't extinct! President Kaesus—" she bit back a hiss as his betrayal reared its ugly head. "He knows they're still alive! He injected me with some sort of serum and removed my memories of my time with the dragons."

I suppose I should be grateful he only wiped my memory. At least he didn't kill me to keep me quiet. I wonder how many others have found the truth and had their memories wiped?

Alistair straightened and met her gaze with shining eyes. "I had my suspicions but no proof. This is good news!" He clapped his hands together before hurrying around his cave, throwing his sparse belongings into a pack. "I have many things to do, and little time to do it in. I won't ask for the whole story, but tell me, have you heard of the Little Birds?"

She hesitated a moment, unsure if she should admit her knowledge out loud, but decided to put her trust in her friend. She nodded mutely and tensed, waiting to see his reaction.

"Thank Ghaia." He continued packing as he spoke, the tips of his stone wings grating against the cave floor. "Go to them. Tell them Greykin sent you and that I've had to flee. I can't say where, but I will send word when I can." He stopped his hurry and joined her in the centre of the cave. Placing his fingertips under her chin, he forced her gaze up to look him in the eye. "You have a bigger role to play than you realise. The Gods sent me a dream months ago that I had to make that dragon for you. I was told it had to be imbued with the magic of a moon crystal. The next day Tormund happened to bring me a moon crystal that he'd discovered on his last expedition. I don't usually dream, so I knew this meant something. I have played my part in the Gods' plan, now you must play yours. There is much change coming. Be ready for it."

That was the most she had ever heard the gargoyle speak. Unsure where to start, Sera stammered over her words. "What do you mean, the Gods' plan? You mean they're real? And no matter what I want, there is a pre-determined design for my life? You've got to be joking."

Alistair smiled sadly and murmured, "You always have a choice."

A wave of déjà vu washed over her as she recalled a similar conversation with Arius after they had become Soulbound. Another tremor rocked the ground as the dragon hunting her flung another fireball at the cave's entrance.

"I assume that's Desamor out there. He's Arius' brother and wants me dead," she explained to Alistair. "He can control the weather, which explains the mist." Sera fingered Firinne's blade lovingly, thankful the gluxxor had recharged its magical properties.

It certainly came in handy today.

"Well," announced Alistair, "I think that's our cue to leave."

Sera shot him a puzzled look. "And how exactly do you propose we do that?"

"I can create a tunnel."

"That will take weeks!" she exclaimed.

"You forget my affinity with the earth. You don't think my ability to make my art so lifelike comes purely from practise, do you? I am a mythic made of stone, and it does my bidding. Just as the earth shapes itself according to my will, it also whispers its secrets to me. How else do you think I came to be in this precise cave when you dropped in?"

Fray piped up from where he'd perched on a rocky outcrop, "Don't forget about me in your plans to get out of here! I don't want to have to deal with an angry dragon alone!"

They both chuckled at the bird's offended tone. Fray fluffed his feathers indignantly.

"Hang on," interrupted Sera before Alistair could perform any magic with the earth. "Fray, weren't you leading me to my nanna before we were attacked? Where is she? I can't leave her to fend for herself with Desamor hanging around."

He bobbed his head energetically then flew to the gargoyle's shoulder. "If I tell you where Del is, can you use your magic to get Sera there?"

Alistair nodded solemnly. Fray paused and his eyes rolled back once more as Del's deep blue eyes took their place. "I'm near a waterfall to the north of my cottage. There's a rowan tree on the east side of the creek. There's a large clump of boulders at the top of the waterfall that resembles a dragon's head."

The stony skin around Alistair's eyes crinkled when he smiled and said, "I know that place."

Fray's eyes turned black again and he hacked out a few hoarse caws. He flew back to Sera's shoulder and sniffed, disgruntled. "I hate it when she does that," he grumbled.

CHAPTER EIGHTEEN

A THUNDERING BELLOW SPLIT the air from above-
ground followed by a loud crash as something enormous
landed on the earth.

"He's here," Sera hissed, fear electrifying her skin.

Without wasting any time, Alistair laid his granite
hand against the cave and closed his eyes. His normally
dull body lit up with flecks of blue light as he called
upon his magic. The rock warped around his hand and
a small crack fractured down the wall. The stone almost
appeared liquid where Alistair's magic coaxed it into
reshaping itself. The crack widened slowly, creating a
passageway out of the cave. Being a gargoyle, Alistair
didn't sweat, but his wings drooped from the effort.

"Go," he commanded.

"What about you? You're not staying here to fight Desamor, are you?" she cried.

"That would be very foolish, not to mention suicidal.
No." He shook his head. "I will follow you for a time and
then collapse my tunnel behind us. When my energy has
returned, I will create another path for my own journey."
He broke off and passed the torch to Sera. "You need this
more than I do." She thanked him, then he added, "Don't
forget to tell the Little Birds about Greykin."

"I won't forget."

"Good. Now go!"

Sera wrapped the gargoyle up in a brief hug, his eyes widening slightly at her unexpected touch, then slipped into the newly-made tunnel with Fray on her shoulder and the torch in her hand. Alistair followed with his pack of supplies. As they exited the cavern a shower of rocks fell from above as Desamor groped inside the top cave, seeking her. Once they were safely ensconced within the channel, Alistair stopped and summoned his magic to close off the entrance. His glowing blue body cast enchanting flecks of light over the uneven walls, reminding Sera of glow worms. She shook her head and turned away; there was no time to admire the magical display.

"Goodbye," she whispered before hurrying down the passage. She moved swiftly, her Tracker training ensuring she remained sure-footed, even on the uneven ground. The torch's bright light cast bizarre patterns on the earthen walls as she jogged. Occasionally, roots of trees broke through the ceiling of the tunnel and Sera had to duck her head to avoid them. They left the frustrated roars of Desamor behind eventually and the silence became deep and heavy. Sera sensed the pressure of the tonnes of dirt above them and a tightness closed around her chest. It reminded her of the last time she was scrambling in a narrow tunnel away from the sounds of Arius and Desamor fighting. She pushed the feeling away and focused on the steady rhythm of her feet pounding against the ground. It was different this time. This time she wasn't crawling forward blindly, hoping she wasn't going to get stuck at a dead end, plus she had company.

"So, Fray," she panted, "I've been going to Nanna's for years and I've never seen you move. Tell me about yourself."

"Why should I?" he harrumphed, irritated by the dirt that periodically trickled from above their heads onto his sleek feathers.

"Because," she wheezed, "I'm trying not to focus on the crushing weight of earth above our heads that is being held in place only by magic. And I'm too puffed to talk about myself."

Fray's chilly demeanour relaxed and he squeezed her shoulder gently with his talons. "Fair enough, fair enough." He bobbed his head a few times as he pondered his next words. "Many years ago, before you were born, Del saved my life. I was one heartbeat away from death and she used a different type of magic to save me. I've been her Guardian since then and have acted as a watcher on her gate when I'm in stasis. I have enough energy left in my body to alert her to an intruder. But, as you learnt today, I need blood to waken properly. Speaking of," he cocked his head, "I will need more blood soon or I will return to my stuffed appearance. Stuffed!" He guffawed loudly, finding some amusement in his predicament, his screeches reverberating down the tunnel.

"Is there any chance you could hold out a while longer? I think we're getting close and I don't really feel like bleeding again today." She huffed out her question as she felt the path gradually rise beneath her feet.

"I can give you an hour."

"I hope that's enough," she muttered. She cursed aloud as she remembered her backpack was still at the cottage.

I guess Nanna will have to go without her groceries this time. And I'll need a new backpack if Desamor keeps hanging around her home.

"Seraphina?" A female voice floated to them from ahead.

"Nanna? Is that you?" Sera called back.

"Thank goodness! Is Fray with you?" Del yelled.

In response, Fray cawed and flapped urgently towards the voice. Sera chuckled softly and jogged a little faster, her breathing coming easier as she felt the ominous weight of the earthen ceiling lift.

"Not far now," her grandmother's Guardian squawked back to her.

Sera burst out of the tunnel into the bright light of the early afternoon sun.

Strange. It feels later than it actually is. Probably hasn't helped that I've been in the dark for the last couple of hours.

She had a brief moment where she noticed the charming sight of the waterfall tumbling into a deep pool and a makeshift hut made of branches and bark sitting beneath a rowan tree, before Del enveloped her in a tight embrace. Sera clutched her desperately and buried her face in her shoulder. Unexpectedly, a wave of sobs wracked her body and she sank into her nanna's arms. She cried for the time she'd lost, for the hostility she'd unfairly flung at Arius and for all the pain and confusion she'd felt since returning to Mandar City. Allowing herself to lean into the emotion, her cries gradually softened and turned into tears of relief at finally remembering everything that had happened to her. The gloom that had stained all her recent thoughts bled away and a newfound peace draped itself over her like a cloak.

Pulling her tear-stained face away from Del, she wiped her cheeks. Clearing her throat, she announced, "I've got my memories back."

The old woman whooped, then grasped the tops of her arms and said, "Tell me everything!"

Sera followed her nanna into the hut where Del prepared a meal of boiled roots, nuts, skyberries and dandelion tea. As the earthy scent of cooking filled the air, she realised just how hungry she was. Fray perched outside the hut and kept watch while he guzzled the blood from the fresh carcass of a rabbit. Sera sat down on a log and recounted everything, from the time when she first joined minds with Arius and his resulting abduction, to the Dragon Council, to the battle between Arius and Desamor. She explained their soulbinding and how they'd been separated during Desamor's storm. Every now and then Del would interrupt with a question but she mostly sat in silence, chewing her lip.

Sera shared the frightening experience of having a nest of hippogryphs ready to execute her if the queen had demanded it and the guilt she'd felt when Torvold had given up his family to save her. She spoke with venom of the harpy pinning her with magic and taking her to the president who had injected her with something to take her memories away. She then gave a brief overview of what had happened since her return to work. At the end of her narrative, she stared into her cooling tea that she cradled in a cup Del had fashioned from bark.

Thinking out loud, she murmured, "I guess that means that the employer the harpy mentioned is President Kaesus. So he doesn't want me dead, but he doesn't want me to remember anything to do with the dragons? Wouldn't it have been easier to kill me and make it look as if I died on my camping trip?"

Her grandmother fondled the locket at her neck as she stared blankly at the inside of the wall made of branches and bark. "It is rather odd. He's a strange man." She glared intently at Sera. "Swear to me, if he crosses your path again, you'll do your best to steer clear of him."

"I will," she promised. "Hey, Nanna, I have a question for you now. When I last saw Idris, he gave me this," she pulled out the Seeing Stone from her pocket, "and said you helped him create it. How is that possible?"

Del looked meaningfully at Sera, almost as if she hoped she would pick up on an ulterior message, but sighed when her granddaughter only gave her a puzzled look. "That's not something I can tell you. Many years ago, I made a blood oath that would protect the people I loved. But in doing so, my tongue has been bound. I can't share the secret. I wish I could tell you why I—" she abruptly cut off and gasped for air as the curse held her tight until she stopped struggling. Rubbing her throat, she said sadly, "I've already lost my daughter because of the truth and I couldn't bear it if I lost you too. The only way you might find out is by guessing it on your own." She arched her grey brows, inviting Sera to solve the mystery.

She nodded slowly and gathered her thoughts. "The only way I can see that you could have helped Idris make the Seeing Stone is by wielding magic yourself. And the only way you could use magic is if you were a mythic." Del nodded along enthusiastically. "Or maybe you could have been granted the power by a mythic? I've never heard of it happening but..." Her nanna was frowning now, so she backtracked. "Okay, so you're a mythic. Or you have mythic blood. Which means that..." she trailed off as she stared at Del in wonder. Her heart pounded in her ears as she whispered the next sentence, "I share the same blood as you. It means we both have magic."

Del clapped her hands together joyfully but didn't say anything.

"Can you tell me which mythic we are related to?"

Shaking her head, Del pointed at her throat.

"I understand." Sera's mind was racing as she mentally ran through a list of humanoid mythics that could have procreated with a person. There weren't many options.

Del pulled her into an unexpected hug and whispered, "It's nice to finally be able to share that with you. I wish I could tell you everything about our lineage. But don't go digging into our family heritage, at least, not for now. It's not safe, especially with President Kaesus watching you."

"That makes sense. I'll be careful."

"Good girl." Del patted her gently on the cheek, her eyes crinkling as she grinned at her granddaughter.

"Nanna, I was wondering, did you receive my text this morning? I never received a response."

"No. I had a feeling I was being watched yesterday morning, so I packed some things and came here. I left my mobile phone at home as I was worried it would make it easier for whoever was stalking me to follow. I had hoped to be home before you noticed I was gone." Her lips twisted in a wry smile.

Sera ran her fingertips absentmindedly over the tender skin in the crook of her elbow. "Which leads me to another question. On my way to find you, when Desamor's mist wrapped around me and halted my progress, you connected to Fray and told me to use Firinne to cut myself free. How did you know that would work?"

Twisting her hands in agitation, her nanna gave a weary sigh. "The knife was originally mine and I passed it onto your mother. When we lost her, your father executed your mother's Will and kept it safe until your graduation. When Firinne was originally forged it was imbued with magic from a particular mythic in our bloodline." She choked on her next words and paused to compose herself. "I can't go into detail but it's because of the way it was forged that it was able to cut through that enchanted mist."

Sera nodded slowly as she processed the information. *It feels like for every answer I uncover, there's a new question that confuses me further.*

Del cupped Sera's chin and pecked her on the cheek, her wrinkled skin brushing against her. "Now, I think it's time you went home so no one thinks you've gone missing again."

CHAPTER NINETEEN

SERA WOVE AN INTRICATE path on her journey home, leaving false trails, walking through creeks and doubling back in an effort to conceal her nanna's location. Del had announced she would hide there for the time being. She claimed it wasn't only Desamor who had been watching her house. She'd purposely left her mobile at the cottage so she couldn't be tracked by her phone's signal. Now it was up to Sera not to lead anyone to Del's temporary home.

There was no sign of Desamor as she hiked back towards Mandar City, so she braved the fields to the south-west of the capital, closer to the cottage, so it wasn't obvious where she'd actually come from. As she trudged through the stalks of wheat, she took the time to sift through every memory and process her experiences. When she thought of Arius, a warmth thrummed through her chest and her palm itched. Finally, the injuries on her body made sense.

Admittedly, I still don't fully understand what it means to be Soulbound, but at least now I know that I'm glad to be bound to Arius.

As she walked towards the first lot of outlying buildings that formed the capital city of Mandar, she decided to test her ability to see the auras of nearby creatures. She hadn't practised her skill since she'd forgotten everything so she realised she couldn't push too hard or she'd end up fainting, like she had the first time.

Not a good idea to pass out with an angry dragon hunting me and without Arius here to take care of me.

She quietened her mind and extended her thoughts into her surroundings. The golden field lit up around her, resembling stars sparkling in the night sky. It was magical. Tiny balls of light shone from the thousands of insects and small rodents that called the field home. As she approached the city, the slightly larger auras of the birds swooping through the sky captured the smaller lights, winking them out of existence as they ate the insects that braved the open air. When she sensed the auras of the nearby farmer and his wife who grew the crops she was walking through, she withdrew her mind.

Sweat beaded her temple after the effort so she paused her march and ate some of the skyberries her nanna had given her. The rare fruit burst with flavour in her mouth, tart yet sweet, and boosted her energy. The daylight was fading as the sun set over the hills at her back. Shrugging her jacket back on, she shivered as the first touch of cool night air licked her skin. She hoped Arius would keep his promise and visit tonight. Leaving the calm of the fields behind, her feet hastily followed the pavement that led to the inner city skyrises that housed her apartment. Her phone buzzed in her pocket, breaking the serenity she had enjoyed for so long. Checking the screen, she saw it was Hazel. Her brows pulled together. Hazel typically texted, it was unusual for her to call.

"Hey, Hazel, what's up?" she answered.

"None of the usual remedies are working!" Hazel exclaimed.

"What are you talking about?"

"Your dad! I went to check on him when I finished work and he's worse. He's considering going to the infirmary at the MRO, but I don't think they have the right medicine to help him. I'm so sorry, Sera, I'm doing everything I can and I will keep trying. I'm back at home now, just figuring out a new remedy to test." She began muttering to herself about herb combinations.

"Shit. Okay. Let me think." Sera stopped walking as she absorbed the unexpected news. "I'll go and see him now. And I'll help get him to the MRO if he decides to go."

"Just be careful. I haven't seen any sign of his illness being infectious but it may take a few days to incubate. I feel fine, but I've been careful to wash my hands and keep the area sterile when I've been around him."

"All right, thanks for the heads up. By the way, Hazel, I figured you'd want to know... I've got my memories back."

"What?" Her friend screeched the word so loudly it made Sera drop her phone. She scooped it up in time to hear her ask, "How?"

"I can't go into it over the phone but everything is great. And Arius is who he says he is. He's my Soulbound." Happiness bubbled up inside, even with the new concern of her father's illness. With her memories returned, she felt like she could handle anything. She felt whole.

"I'm so happy for you, Sera! That's amazing. I can't wait to hear about it all. I'll see how I go with this mixture and either come to visit Allen tonight, or first thing tomorrow. Could you tell me how he's doing when you get there?"

"Can do. Thanks, Hazel. Talk soon."

Sera hung up and paused for a moment to get her bearings. She was on the sidewalk near Tregua Park, meaning the quickest way to reach her father's apartment was to cross the park and head up Barrow Street. She walked quickly across the manicured lawn, not taking the time she usually did to admire the beautiful yellow blooms of the Peace Tree. A three-note whistle sounded from above her, faltering her determined march.

It's just one of the birds that live in the park, stop being so jumpy.

The distinctive tune sounded again, making the hair stand up on the nape of her neck. She had a disturbing feeling she was being watched. She instinctively sank into her meditative state and cast her mind out, ignoring the bugs that swirled through the night air. A human aura glowed in the boughs of the Peace Tree and she gasped. Spinning away to avoid being attacked from above, she pulled Firinne out, ready to defend herself if necessary.

The leaves above where she'd just been standing rustled and a young boy dropped from the branches, landing catlike on the grass. He looked to be around nine-years-old but it was hard to tell for sure as he was a skinny, wretched looking thing. Her heart broke when she noticed the dark circles under his eyes and the permanently pained expression on his face. His dark hair stuck up at odd angles and his clothing was thin. He studied her with narrowed eyes. She returned her blade to its sheath and held her hands up to show she was unarmed. Something about his face niggled at her; he seemed familiar although she couldn't think why.

"You're not a squab, are you?" the boy demanded hostilely as he studied her. "You don't look like one."

"A squab? What's that?"

"A guard. From the IRC?" He looked at her as if she was stupid. "On the street, we call them squabs. As in squabblers."

"I haven't heard that nickname before," said Sera. Squabblers were furry little mythics whose cute appearance betrayed a nasty habit of attacking passersby and draining their blood.

His eyes brightened unexpectedly. "You're the one they told me to look for," he said matter-of-factly. He pointed a bony finger at her chest, making her glance down, mystified. The necklace with the carved wooden bird that Helena had given her was now sitting on top of her shirt. It must have fallen out when she leant down to pick up her phone from the ground.

"Oops!" she exclaimed and tucked it back under her shirt hurriedly before asking, "Who are you?"

"I'm Wren."

"Nice to meet you, Wren. I'm Sera." She scrutinised his face and realised why she recognised him. "You're the boy from the market! The one who nearly got crushed by that tauron!"

He blinked at her with wide brown eyes before replying slowly, "You're the one who saved me."

"I wish you had let me help more. Here, have these." She pulled out the rest of the skyberries from her jacket. They wouldn't last him long but it was better than noth-ing. He cautiously slunk towards her and snatched the berries before leaping back and stuffing his face.

"So, who do you mean when you said 'they' told you to look for me?"

Purple juice dribbled down his chin when he replied, "The Little Birds." He swallowed before adding, "They want to meet you."

"How do I find them?"

"Look for the sign."

"You're the second person to tell me that. Problem is, I don't know what the sign looks like!"

"The bird on your necklace. That's their symbol. It's drawn above an entry to the sewers over there." He gestured to a point over her shoulder. "Follow the birds and they will lead you to them."

"That's very helpful, thank you, Wren." He blinked rapidly at her. Something told her he wasn't used to receiving kind words. She glanced at the time on her PSB and winced. "I have to be somewhere now, but I will find them tomorrow, okay?" He nodded and backed away from her. With one impressive leap he caught hold of a low branch and scampered into the cover of the Peace Tree.

CHAPTER TWENTY

AS SHE EXITED TREGUA Park, Sera texted her father to say she was coming over. As the minutes ticked by without a reply, her apprehension grew. An unexpected sensation of comfort intruded on her fretting, making her wonder whether her Soulbound was nearby. She cast her mind out once more and felt his presence concealed high in the clouds above.

Arius?

Seraphina? The delight that coloured his voice was infectious and she couldn't help but smile.

My memories have returned. I remember everything!

He roared, words unable to adequately capture his joy.

She interrupted his rejoicing. *There will be time for a proper celebration later. I need your help. My father, Allen, is unwell and I'm worried it's something serious. Do you think you can hold your human form long enough to come to his home with me and see whether there's something you can do?*

Of course, my love. The closer I am to you, the easier it is to locate your soul so it won't be a problem for me to find you. However, I won't risk flying into the city, I will land in the forest and meet you at his home.

Good idea. Press the intercom button for apartment number 57 when you get to the front door and I'll buzz you in.

I do not understand what that means but I'm sure I will figure it out. His warm chuckle eased her anxiety further.

Just find the panel beside the front door. Press the button beside number 57. I will press the button in my dad's apartment and it will let you in the front door. When you get to the elevator, press the button with the 5 on it. See you soon.

She broke off their mental link and made her way up the steps to the front door of her father's complex. She still had access since she used to live there, and they'd never bothered to have her access removed since she frequently came over for dinner. Scanning her PSB, she let herself into the foyer. Striding across the polished concrete floor, she entered the waiting elevator. Tapping her foot impatiently, she watched the numbers tick slowly upward. Finally, the doors opened and she sprinted down the hall to Allen's apartment. As she reached her hand out to unlock it, she realised the door was slightly ajar. Worrying her lip, she slowly pushed the door open and peeked into the lounge. The lights had been left on and exposed the chaos left behind by what appeared to be a burglary. She bit back a gasp as she entered and automatically unsheathed Firinne.

Stepping carefully over the contents of the emptied kitchen drawers, she called out, "Dad! Are you here?"

There was no answer. She stayed close to the walls as she moved through the apartment in case the thief was still there and waiting to attack. The silence was leaden. Recognising her energy levels were low, she made the conscious decision to sweep the area with her mind to ensure there was no one else there. Dropping back into her meditative state, she sensed there were no other life forms within her father's apartment. Releasing her power, her strength drained from her body and her face paled as she propped herself against the lounge room wall. She hadn't used her gift to sense auras and connect with Arius for over a week and the effort of using it multiple times today had fatigued her terribly.

She rummaged frantically in her jacket pocket before remembering she'd given the last of her skyberries to Wren. She slid down the wall, her face clammy as she lifted trembling hands to her cheeks. Her world continued to spin so she laid her head against the cool floor tiles while she waited for the dizziness to pass. Eventually, her energy grew enough for her to attempt to stand. Using the couch for support, Sera pulled herself into an upright position. Her feet were splayed out like a newborn foal and it took her a few more minutes to regain her balance.

Thank the Gods there wasn't anyone here. I would've been screwed if the intruder had still been here and attacked.

A piercing screech sounded and she winced at the shattered silence. She slowly stumbled over to the intercom, taking care not to step on her father's belongings that littered the floor, and buzzed Arius into the complex. She couldn't summon the energy to link her mind to his so she just waited for him to arrive. It didn't take long before he was striding down the hallway that led to apartment number 57. She smiled weakly and held the front door open, pleased to see him even through her exhaustion. He returned her smile and cupped her face in his hands. Staring deep into her eyes, the joy radiating from his soul was palpable. He kissed her tenderly and leant his forehead against hers, his familiar scent and loving touch immediately soothing her worries. Too soon, he leant away and scrutinised her expression.

"What's wrong?" he asked, his fingertips still tracing her cheek. "Is your father awfully unwell?" Before she could answer, he peered past her and hissed at the chaos. "Gods! Someone has broken into his home? Where is he now? Did they take anything?"

"I'm not sure." She brushed a tired hand through her hair, realising there were dirt and twigs stuck in her tresses from her mad dash through the forest and tunnel. Surreptitiously, she tried to brush the worst of it out without Arius noticing. He stalked through the lounge and disappeared down the hallway. While he checked the rest of the apartment, Sera pulled her phone out.

He might have gone to the infirmary and someone has broken in after he's left. She didn't want to think about what might have happened if he was still home when the burglar had arrived. . She phoned her father but when it went straight to his messagebank, she called the MRO.

"Thank you for calling the after-hours service centre of the Mythic Relations Office. This is Quill speaking, can I help you?"

Sera stammered over her first words, since it was normally Marjorie or Dylan who manned the after-hours phonelines. She'd never heard of Quill. "Hi, it's Sera here. I mean, Tracker Seraphina. Was I speaking with Quill?"

"Yes," he replied pleasantly. "How can I help you, Tracker Seraphina?"

"I was just wondering whether you could tell me if my father has checked into the infirmary? His name is Tracker Allen Azura."

"Certainly, let me find out for you. Please hold the line," Quill purred. A short wait and he was back. "Yes, Tracker Allen is being taken care of in the infirmary."

"Thank the Four Gods! I'll be right over."

"I'm sorry, you can't access the infirmary outside of visiting hours." Quill's voice was gentle but firm.

"I need to see my father," she pleaded.

"I'm sorry, but that's impossible. Visiting hours are from nine am until seven pm. Tracker Allen is currently asleep, but I will ask the medic to have him contact you as soon as he wakes tomorrow. If his condition changes overnight, we'll be in touch."

Sera released a frustrated exhale. "Fine. Thank you." She sagged against the doorframe.

"My pleasure, take care now." He hung up.

Sera quickly reported the break-in on DOPL's website before messaging Hazel to say Allen was at the infirmary. After Hazel replied saying she would visit him in the morning, Sera glanced up from her phone and realised Arius was standing in front of the couch now, watching her. She gave him a wobbly grin and explained, "Dad's gone to the MRO infirmary. He's sleeping now so I'll let him rest and head over in the morning."

"He's in good hands, Sera. I'm sure they'll take care of him there."

"I know. I just wish I could see him for myself."

"There's nothing more you can do," he soothed. "He can rest easy there. Speaking of rest, you need some. Did you want to sleep here?"

Sera looked at the mess and shook her head. "It doesn't feel right being here without Dad. Plus, what if the thief comes back?"

Arius chuckled at that. "I think I could protect you from a simple thief. But I can understand your reluctance." He studied her and cocked his head. "I sensed your aura moving outside the city limits today. Where did you go?

"I went to visit my nanna, but Desamor found me first."

"What?" Arius exclaimed. "Did he hurt you?"

"No. I'm fine." She shoved herself off the doorframe and, closing the gap between them, laid a placating hand against his arm. "I had help from some friends and escaped. Alistair, a gargoyle, fashioned the underground tunnel to take me to Nanna and then her Guardian, a raven named Fray, led me to her. She disappeared into the woods yesterday when she sensed Desamor watching her cottage."

Arius shifted anxiously but offered her a reluctant smile. "She sounds like a smart woman. I'm glad you found her safely. We must stay alert in case Desamor tries to hunt you down again. Will you allow me to escort you home?"

"I'd like that," she said and linked her arm through his. Her lips lifted in pleasure at the warmth radiating from his emerald eyes as he ran his gaze over her body. He noticed her smile and smirked before pressing a chaste kiss to her cheek and leading her out of the apartment.

When they entered the elevator, he watched her closely as she pressed the button for the ground floor. He cocked his head and said, "That took me a little bit to work out when I was running to you. I didn't realise you had to press the button outside the door first. I nearly ripped the doors open myself. Luckily, a faun was coming up at the same time and did it for me. He certainly gave me a strange look."

Sera began giggling, which led into a long belly-laugh, the kind she hadn't had for a long time. Something about imagining a great dragon, masquerading as a human, attempting to operate an elevator, was ridiculously comical.

"Do I amuse you?" Arius growled. The gravelly tone in his voice caused her core to clench and her breath to hitch. The temperature in the lift rose when he met her gaze, his irises pooling liquid green. He pushed her against the wall, grabbing her hands and raising them above her head. "Answer me, Seraphina. Do you find my blunder humorous?" Arius covered her mouth with his, suffocating any answer she might have given. He traced the line of her jaw with hot kisses, his breath whispering over her skin. She couldn't think straight as his body pressed against hers and his lips worked their way down her neck to her collarbone. She whimpered with desire when he paused there and ran his nose along her shoulder. He let out a heavy sigh and stepped away reluctantly as the elevator doors pinged open.

"Don't take this the wrong way, Seraphina, but I adore the way you smell."

She burst out laughing again. "Why would I find that offensive?"

"Well, the last time I tried to say nice things about you at your apartment, I thought you were going to throat-punch me."

She went on her tip-toes and pressed a soft kiss to his lips. "That was before I got my memories back. You wouldn't want me kissing anybody who complimented me, would you?"

His brows pulled low and he grumbled, "That's true."

She linked her arm through his again and they journeyed towards her home, delighting in the cool night air. As they walked, Sera filled him in on everything that had happened to her since they'd been separated. When they arrived at the main door to her complex, he stopped.

"I won't come up. It's late and you need your rest." She opened her mouth to argue but he held a hand up to interrupt her. "But never fear, I won't be far away. I will keep watch from above tonight. I will see you again tomorrow."

Realisation dawned and she spoke her thoughts aloud, "That wasn't a dream last night, was it? Even though I didn't remember you or my gift, my mind automatically connected with you. Just like the first time."

He smiled warmly and pulled her into his arms, laying his head atop hers. "That's right. It made me so happy to speak with you, even if you didn't understand what was happening. But I am overjoyed now that you have recovered your memories. I can't tell you how happy it makes me to be with you again. I've been so worried."

Sera's face dropped in self-reproach. She'd been so caught up in her own world that she hadn't given any thought to how Arius must have felt when he lost her at Lake Eyre. She hadn't even asked him what had happened to him since they were separated.

"Don't." He kissed her forehead. "You don't need to worry about my feelings."

"I thought you couldn't hear my thoughts unless I projected them to you?"

"I can't," he laughed. "But your face is an open book. I see the shadow of guilt in your expression. We will need to have a good, long talk soon about everything that has happened. But not tonight. You need sleep. Rest easy. Your father is safe at the infirmary, your memories are back and I am here. All is well. Fly fierce, my love."

She recalled his sister, Aliah, saying the same thing to him when they'd parted. Recalling his returning comment, she smiled and said, "Strike strong, Arius."

He beamed at her, thrilled by her desire to acknowledge his culture. He kissed the top of her hand and strode away down the street. The pain of their parting was softened by the heat of his lips that remained burning on her skin.

CHAPTER TWENTY-ONE

BALANCING HER MORNING COFFEE in one hand, Sera staggered to Tregua Park with her arms full. She had a blanket, a few bottles of fresh water, plus a couple of blueberry muffins and a loaf of bread, all still warm from the baker's oven. She stumbled over to the Peace Tree and laid the goods at the foot of it. Attempting to imitate the tune Wren had whistled to her, she scanned the foliage. Dark eyes peeped out at her from behind the deep green leaves and an answering whistle sounded, but the boy refused to exit the tree. Glancing around, Sera realised there were quite a few beings hurrying along the pavement already, travelling to work.

I suppose Wren wants to stay hidden. He certainly wouldn't want to be found by a squab. Her lips lifted in amusement at the nickname he had for the IRC guards.

Leaving her bundled offering nestled in the tree roots, she turned around and walked towards the area Wren had gestured to last night. The infirmary wouldn't allow her in for another two hours so she figured she may as well search for the Little Birds to keep herself from worrying about her father. As she exited the park, she kept her eyes peeled for the image of a bird that mimicked the one on Helena's necklace. She'd never really paid attention to the sewers before and wondered what the entrance might look like. Scanning the pavement for some sort of manhole, she turned a corner onto a quiet side street and stumbled across a grate. It was lucky that she even saw it as it was the same shade of grey as the concrete in which it was set. A small chalk drawing of a bird was sketched beside it, making Sera grin, confident this was the entry Wren had told her about.

She propped herself nonchalantly against the building until she was certain no one was looking. Leaning down, she hastily slid the grate open. Peering into the hole, she pulled her phone out of her pocket, turned the torch on and shone it into the sewer. A ladder hugged the wall closest to her, making it easy to descend into the tunnel. Putting her phone away, she swiftly swung in, and looping one arm around a rail for balance, pulled the grate closed above her head. The rails were slippery and the air was damp so she took her time climbing down. Landing softly on the concrete floor, her triumph quickly turned to dismay.

How am I supposed to find the Little Birds? There's nothing here!

The empty shaft stretched ahead interminably with more tunnels branching off to each side. The dim sunlight of dawn dappled through other grates at random intervals in front of her, creating a patchwork of light and dark. Shivering in the cool, she pulled her jacket tight around her. It was then that she noticed another chalk drawing of the bird on the wall beside the rails. Its beak pointed in the opposite direction so she turned around. Wren's instructions were to follow the birds so she decided to start walking and see whether it led to anything. There was a narrow channel in the centre of the tunnel where dirty water ran in the same direction as she was moving. Wrinkling her nose, Sera did her best to ignore the stench.

After what seemed like an eternity, she noticed another bird chalked on the entrance to a narrow side passage. The bird was facing down the tunnel so Sera skipped over the foul-smelling water and sidled down the new path, following the bird's directions. It was much darker in here, with fewer grates letting in the sun, so she pulled her phone out again and turned the torch back on. The new tunnel had many twists and turns compared to the main sewer. She found and followed two more birds chalked on the wall.

As time wore on and she didn't find any new signs, she wondered whether she'd missed something and was lost underground. Feeling thoroughly confused and chilled to the bone, Sera contemplated turning back and finding her way home. Panic flared in her chest at the thought of being trapped in the tunnels, but she shoved it down and focused on placing one foot in front of the other on the damp concrete. Just as she was ready to give up, another bird finally presented itself. This one was styled differently to the others, with its wings spread wide and its head pointing upward.

Sera released a sigh of relief when she noticed the ladder beside it, leading to a manhole in the ceiling. Tucking her phone in her jacket pocket she climbed to the top of the rails. Leaning out she pushed her shoulder against the metal circle and groaned at the weight. Slowly the covering lifted and she managed to shove it sideways. The hole was positioned a little too far away from the rails to allow her to easily view the room she was about to enter. After nearly fainting in her father's apartment yesterday, she was hesitant to use her power again so soon.

What if I'm still weakened? I can't afford to go into the Little Birds' nest without having all my wits about me. I'd rather go in not knowing who's there and be able to fight, than go in and pass out before I'm even attacked.

With one hand holding on, she pulled her phone out and shone its torch into the darkness above her. She couldn't make anything out so turned it off and tucked it back in her pocket. A shiver of trepidation prickled over her skin as she wondered what she would find on the other side.

Who are the Little Birds? What's their purpose? She glowered at the dark room through the opening for a moment longer before sighing in defeat. *If Alistair and Helena trust them, then so do I.*

She reached out from the top rail again and grabbed the near side of the opening. Letting go of the ladder, she scrabbled against the side of the wall with her feet to push herself through. Her torso was on a dirt floor but her legs were still dangling when someone grabbed the back of her jacket and bodily lifted her out of the hole. In the next moment, she was flung through the air and struck a wall, where all the air left her body. She fumbled for Firinne as she sucked in short gasps and tried to find her feet. Before Sera managed to pull her knife out, the shadowy figure pushed her hard against the floor and held her down with his large paws.

"State your name and business here!" the male voice demanded.

Sera struggled to speak but could only wheeze as her lungs protested loudly from the blow. Her attacker must have realised this and lessened the weight of his paws before asking again.

"Your name!"

"Seraphina," she gurgled. She debated saying her full name, including her title, but wondered whether an unknown Tracker would be welcomed into their hideout.

She opted to keep that information private for now and added, "I have a message from Greykin. And Wolfseye gave me this." With difficulty, she pulled out Helena's necklace from where it hid beneath her shirt and held the wooden carving up, unsure if her assailant could see it in the dark.

Upon her unveiling, the weight of the paws disappeared, but then a distinctly canine jaw seized the back of her jacket and dragged her along the floor.

"I can walk!" she protested loudly and he huffed at her indignation. "I swear, I don't mean anyone here any harm."

The grip on her jacket released and a door ahead of her opened, flooding the room with artificial light.

"Stay here," the wolfish mythic growled and stalked out the door, shutting it behind him.

Sera heard the squawk of a two-way radio and a female voice responding to him through the door as she stood up and dusted herself off. The small room she found herself in was empty aside from the metal covering she'd pushed open, that now lay on the dirt floor she'd already become acquainted with. The log walls and sloping iron roof with exposed beams suggested this might be one of the old buildings that had been condemned after the Mythic War. The door opened then, and the canine mythic jerked his head, summoning her. She exited the tiny room into a massive space. Sera blinked in the bright light and waited for her eyes to adjust. The dated building style remained the same, but desks, monitors, armour and weapons filled the area, along with a few humans and mythics who were studying a map on one of the monitors. One of the humans noticed Sera entering and hurriedly swiped the screen, removing the map from sight.

Studying the mythic who was leading her to one end of the building, she realised he was a werewolf. A thrill of fear raced through her. Most werewolves she'd heard of had gone rogue from their bloodlust, hunting other large mythics such as unicorns and hippogryphs. His head was nearly as tall as her shoulder and, while his shaggy tan coat softened his appearance, it couldn't hide his eerie human-like eyes or the fangs jutting from his jaws. He glanced at her and must have noticed her apprehension.

"So long as you're a friend of the Little Birds, you have nothing to fear from me." His tongue lolled out in a friendly smile and he padded companionably beside her. "I'm Constantine. We've been waiting to meet you, Tracker Seraphina. Your name keeps popping up in the most unlikely of places and our leader wishes to meet you to see whether we can help each other."

"Nice to meet you, Constantine," Sera said, doing her best to mask her residual panic. *Apparently, they already know I'm a Tracker.* "Who is your leader?"

"You'll meet her in a moment."

"Fair enough. Can you tell me what the Little Birds actually do?"

"I think it would be best if I left it up to Urma to explain everything to you. Here," he said with a nudge of his wet nose on her hand. "We're going up here."

He bounded up a wide wooden stairway, each landing making the stairs creak under his weight. He stopped when he reached the second level and waited patiently for her. His warm brown eyes twinkled merrily as she ran after him, doing her best to keep up. With another chuff of laughter, he led her along the wooden platform that ran the perimeter of the second storey. Sera's brow knitted as she realised there were some windows on this level, but all the glass had been painted black. Doors led off the walkway at different points but Constantine ignored these and kept padding along the floorboards until they reached a dead end. He pointed his black nose upward, towards the rafters of the old building. A shadowy figure lounged on one of the beams, cloaked in darkness. A narrow wooden ladder extended from the ceiling to rest at Sera's feet.

Constantine bumped her with his furry head. "Urma awaits you."

She shrugged and clambered up the rungs. Once she reached the top, she picked her way carefully over the interlocking beams toward the stranger.

"Hello," she announced, "I'm Tracker Seraphina Azura."

The mythic rose gracefully from its resting place. A lion's tail snaked out and opened a blacked-out window, allowing the light to fall on her form, exposing her identity. She was a sphinx. The woman's head that sat atop the body of a lioness was hauntingly beautiful. But where her wings should have been, were two stumps.

CHAPTER TWENTY-TWO

SERA GASPED, BEFORE CLAPPING a hand over her mouth, dismayed at her obvious reaction to the amputations. She'd never met a sphinx in her life, as they tended to live in the deserts on Harongar Isle, and now she was bound to have offended this one.

"Appalling, isn't it?" murmured the sphinx gravely, her eyes remaining downcast. Her accent had a musical lilt to it that kept Sera transfixed. "My name is Urma. This atrocity was done to me by your people. When I arrived in Mandar, I was captured and labelled rogue. I was taken to the Iniques Rehabilitation Centre and told I would receive counselling. Instead, they took my greatest joy from me." She flexed the remnants of her wings, the mutilated bronze flesh scarred, a few feathers still attached. "I was released but I buried my shame for years. Too humiliated to allow anyone to see my deformity, I hid in the mountains. But, even though I can no longer take to the air, the wind told me stories." The sphinx approached Sera confidently, not needing to look where she placed her paws on the narrow beams. "There were others like me, who had been taken advantage of, experimented on, tortured. I decided to help them. That's why I founded the Little Birds. To fight back against the humans who would hurt us. To stand up for our rights. To stop this from happening to anyone ever again."

Sera bowed her head in respect. "I'm so sorry. That is a noble cause. I hope you don't mind my impertinence, but I had never heard of the Little Birds until this week. I don't doubt your word, but the IRC is there to help guide rogue mythics and humans back to law-abiding lives. They don't torture anyone."

"That is what they want you to believe, Seraphina. And they do a good job of hiding the truth. I can't prove anything to you with my words alone. And you can't prove to me that you are worthy of my trust yet. But actions speak louder than words. We are in the midst of preparations to conduct an extraction from the IRC of one of our members and now it seems Wolfseye wants us to know we can trust you." Urma inclined her head towards the wooden carving around Sera's neck.

"Why do you call Tracker Helena 'Wolfseye'?" Sera interrupted.

"We use codenames for all of our Little Birds who are working undercover," Urma explained. "Helena is our wolf keeping an eye on the sheep within the MRO. Hence, Wolfseye."

"Got it. So, what do you want from me?"

"I like you." The sphinx smiled, revealing two elongated canines. "You don't mince your words. What we would ask is for you to steal the latest blueprints of the IRC. From what our Little Birds have said, the only copy currently in Mandar City is saved to President Kaesus' Personal Security Band. We need you to steal it for us."

"That's impossible! I can't do that. Why can't Tracker Helena steal it?"

"She has recently fallen under close scrutiny by the President so she is not performing any jobs for us until his attention shifts."

Sera ran her fingers over her hair uneasily. "It's just... I'm trying to avoid the President at the moment, considering the last time we met he obliterated over a week's worth of memories. I have a feeling he won't be so lenient this time."

Urma considered Sera for a long moment with her head cocked, her blonde locks cascading over her shoulders, before saying, "It's for Tormund. He was taken by the IRC and hasn't been seen for weeks. He has been a good friend to the Little Birds over the years. I will do all that I can to save him."

"Professor Tormund's been taken?" she whispered in horror.

"Yes. Because he dared to share the truth about dragons."

"You know they're not extinct?" Sera exclaimed.

"As do you, apparently?" The sphinx's feline ears perked up and her yellow eyes sharpened.

Sera chuckled darkly. "You could say that. That was why President Kaesus removed my memories."

"I see. That's very interesting. And I take it you have them back now?"

"Yes. Alistair— I mean, Greykin — helped return them to me." Absentmindedly, Sera rubbed her arm where the stone dragon had mauled her. It had healed surprisingly fast. The skin was still tender but only a pinkish scar remained.

Urma nodded decisively and said, "This cements my belief that you are the right person for the job."

"How in Ghaia's name would I even begin to try stealing his PSB?"

"The President will be giving a speech at the Choosing Ceremony tomorrow night. Perhaps you could find a way to steal it whilst he's distracted?" Sera opened her mouth to argue but Urma cut her off. "I would appreciate it if you would think on it. Meet Wren at the Peace Tree before the new moon rises tonight and give him your answer. He will tell me your decision."

Sera chewed her lip. "All right then. I'll think about it. By the way, I have a message for the Little Birds. Greykin asked me to tell you that he's had to flee. He didn't say where, but he'll be in contact when it's safe."

"I had been told his cover was blown but when I hadn't heard from him I feared the worst. That's good news that he's safe, at least for now. Thank you for passing his message on. Now, it's time for you to return to Mandar City. A warning for you, Seraphina. Prove yourself trustworthy and we will welcome you into our ranks with open arms. Betray us and you will die. Wolfseye is aware of your task. She'll be watching you closely. If you choose not to accept the mission, you must swear on your life that you won't disclose any information you have learned here. The Little Birds are everywhere and they whisper in my ears. If you deceive us, we will find you." Urma's face lit up with a stunning smile then and she purred, "However, I'm sure you will prove yourself and I won't need to follow through with any of my threats. And don't forget, it is Tormund's life on the line."

CHAPTER TWENTY-THREE

CHECKING THE TIME ON her PSB, Sera grunted in frustration when she realised she still had an hour until the infirmary allowed visitors. As she strode towards the MRO, she phoned her father. Once again, the call went straight to voicemail. Worry settled in the pit of her stomach and, even though she'd be there in ten minutes, she called the MRO.

Quill answered cheerily but with a trace of fatigue from nearing the end of his night shift.

Sera cut him off. "Hi Quill, it's Tracker Seraphina again, can you please put me through to my father in the infirmary?"

"I'll see what I can do," he replied.

Sera marched doggedly on, impatiently waiting for the warm voice of her father to greet her. Disappointment crashed over her when it was Quill who picked up the line again.

"I'm sorry, Tracker Seraphina. He's just in getting some tests done with the medical team and is unavailable to speak. He should be back in his room shortly after nine am."

Sera snarled a curse before asking, "How is he? Can you at least tell me that?"

Quill replied sympathetically, "I'm sorry but the medic didn't say. I'm sure they can answer all of your questions when you arrive."

Hanging up, Sera pounded each step into the sidewalk, her skin prickling with nervous energy. Before long, she entered her workplace and automatically signed in with a touch of her PSB at one of the terminals. She glanced at the empty front desk and raised an eyebrow, surprised not to see Quill there.

It would have been good to put a face to the name.

Her eyes slid up and traced over the sleek silvery letters behind the desk, where the familiar slogan proclaimed that the Mythic Relations Office 'fostered mythic-human relations for a harmonious world.' Switching her focus to her meeting with the Little Birds, she contemplated Urma's request.

Am I really considering stealing from the President? But if I don't steal the plans, and the Little Birds go in there without current information, they'll probably die and Tormund won't be saved.

She mindlessly walked past the elevator she'd usually take to the third floor and followed a hallway towards the rear of the building. She would spend the remainder of the hour before nine am training, in the hopes the exercise would clear her mind and help her come to a decision about the Little Birds' request. Reaching an opaque glass door on the right side of the hall, she swiped her PSB against the control panel and the door slid open with a hiss. She entered the locker room shared by both Hunters and Trackers as the lights automatically turned on.

Sera strode across the tiled floor to her locker and opened it with another tap of her wristband. The tidy shelves inside housed her set of throwing knives, her kurrtoh, a safe that housed her gun and bullets, a spare uniform and her standard-issue MRO Survival Kit. She didn't know how they did it as she never saw cleaners, but a fresh uniform would be in her locker next time she came to train. A single photo of her and Allen at her Choosing Ceremony was pasted to the back wall of the locker.

Her anxiety flared as she felt the pressure building from all the people who were relying on her. Stamping her worries down, she decided not to focus on target practise today, instead grabbing her kurrtoh. The short, unassuming black stick wasn't usually her weapon of choice, but today she needed to sweat. Skimming her finger over a hidden button, the stick elongated into a stave. Hefting it in her hands to refamiliarise herself with the weight, she twirled it around her body once before slinging it over her shoulder and heading to the training yard.

Panting, Sera swung the kurrtoh into the metal dummy again and again. The hum of adrenaline coursing through her veins kept her pushing through the fatigue even as her arms grew heavy. Sweat dripped down her back, drenching her shirt in the heat of the sun. She spun and twisted around the model of the werewolf, landing strikes on its muzzle, spine and legs, as she'd been trained to do. All Hunters and Trackers were taught how to fight mythics with a variety of weapons, with the goal to incapacitate, rather than execute. The MINATH mantra, "Capture, don't kill," was drilled into them from day one of their apprenticeship.

She continued to jab the dummy, her body drained of energy, but her frenzied thoughts had finally calmed. As she leapt away, evading an imaginary attack, Sera realised she'd taken herself into the same meditative place in her mind as when she used her powers. She swept her kurrtoh up under the werewolf's silver jaw, but her fatigue caused the angle of her swing to veer awkwardly. When her stave connected with the metal, it sent shockwaves up her arm. The jarring set her teeth on edge and left a numb feeling in her forearm. Halting her furious attack, she straightened and backed away, rubbing her right arm. Her legs trembled and her body sagged as her battle fury ebbed.

I'll have a shower, then I'll go visit Dad at the infirmary.

Ignoring the other Hunters and Trackers who were now practising in the training yard while she'd focused on her own drill, she headed back to the locker room. The glass door slid closed smoothly behind her and the AI, Frank, said something which she didn't hear but the tone sounded like a question. Sera pulled herself out of her reverie and asked, "Sorry, Frank, what did you say?"

"I said, you seem distracted. Are you well, Tracker Seraphina?"

"Oh! Um…" Frank had never asked her a direct question before, and certainly not one about feelings. He usually announced any arrivals to the office of the Director and was permanently on hand to answer questions from staff. "I'm okay. There's just a lot going on in my head at the moment." A click from the door announced it had been locked and the lights in the locker room blinked out. Fear spiked through Sera and she asked apprehensively, "Erm, Frank? What's happening?"

"I've been wanting to speak to you alone and haven't had an opportunity until now."

The computerised tone of his voice had few inflections, making it difficult to comprehend the context of his words. Sera waited anxiously for him to enlighten her.

"As you know, I see everything in this building. I'm privy to many private conversations. I've spoken to

Tracker Helena and she's asked if I could assist you. I can help you get the President's plans tomorrow night while he's busy at the Choosing Ceremony."

"What? How do you know about that?" she exclaimed.

"As I said, I am working with Tracker Helena. She can't afford to arouse any more suspicion so she's laying low. She mentioned you might be tasked with this job."

"How could you help?"

"I can unlock any door in this building. When the President checks in, I can run a scan on his Personal Security Band claiming it is part of my security process and create a copy of the plans. If you can get to the MRO's secure server during the night, I can transfer it onto your PSB and from there you can give it to the Little Birds."

"Why would you do all this for me?"

"I may only be a computer to you, but I have feelings too. I have seen some terrible things happen to mythics over the years and I want to help put a stop to it."

"How do I know I can trust you?" Sera demanded.

"I suppose you don't. It may help your decision to know that Tracker Helena has entrusted me with her code-name, Wolfseye. I can also tell you, do not use the elevator to access the basement where my Server Room is, as it has a security camera installed. Ultimately, it is your decision whether you place your faith in me and allow me to prove myself when I transfer you the plans."

Sera warred internally. Frank's solution would make her job a lot easier but she wondered whether to trust the AI. She talked out the possible scenarios in her head to weigh up her options.

If I don't accept this job from the Little Birds, Tormund and his rescue team will likely die without the updated IRC plans. If I accept the job and place my trust in Frank, there's a higher chance we'll be successful, meaning none of us die. If he betrays me, then it's the same result as before. No matter how scared I am, I can't just leave Professor Tormund locked up in there.

Mind made up, she said, "If Tracker Helena trusts you, then so do I. Your help would be greatly appreciated. Thank you, Frank."

"You're welcome. If you would hold your PSB over the locker room control panel, I will pinpoint the precise location of my server room so you can find it easily tomorrow night."

Sera did as she was asked and waited until she heard a beep. She tapped her screen and brought up the map of the MRO that she'd received when she commenced her employment. A small red dot that wasn't there previously pulsed in the basement.

"Once the President is giving his speech, sneak away to my server room and I will be able to securely download the file onto your PSB. Do you have any questions?"

"No, I think I've got it."

"If you have any trouble along the way, I may be able to help. Just say my name." Sera could have sworn the tone of Frank's computerised voice almost had a smile in it.

"Thank you," she said sincerely. "This will be an enormous help."

The lights hummed back to life and the door clicked as Frank unlocked it once more. Sera placed her kurrtoh back in the locker and grabbed her spare uniform and a towel before proceeding to the shower. Locking the cubicle door behind her, she undressed and turned the hot water on. As she stepped under the spray, the locker room door hissed open. Paying no mind, Sera continued washing her body until an unwelcome voice began complaining loudly.

"It's so annoying. I just want to get back out there chasing mythics! I wish the stupid bitch would just get over herself," Tyler's voice was unmistakable. Sera's blood ran cold at the sound.

Another Hunter answered, "What's the go with her, anyway? She's not injured, is she? Why is she still stuck on desk duty?"

"Apparently, she went crazy while she was lost in the woods." Sera could almost hear the eyeroll in his voice. "She doesn't remember anything. But that's not my problem! She needs to do her job. I'm sick of spending my days doing odd jobs and target practise. I need to hunt!"

"I get that, man!" The clap of a high-five echoed through the room. Sera kept silent as the hot water ran over her shoulders, praying they didn't take too long so she wouldn't have to face Tyler.

"And another thing," said Tyler. "On Tuesday, when we were tracking the rogue unicorn, a harpy attacked us. She knew Sera. Sera reckons she doesn't have any memory of her, but I think something is going on. And I'm going to find out exactly what it is," he added darkly.

"If Sera is doing something dodgy, you'll figure it out," said Tyler's friend.

"Come on, man, let's forget about her and go shoot some shit."

Two pairs of footsteps exited the locker room. As soon as the door hissed shut, Sera let out an explosive breath and turned off the shower. She dried and dressed herself swiftly before exiting the cubicle and throwing her sweaty uniform into the laundry chute in the wall. She hurried down the hall away from the training yard, glancing over her shoulder to make sure Tyler wasn't there, and added another worry to her growing list.

What am I supposed to tell people now that I have my memories back?

CHAPTER TWENTY-FOUR

SERA ARRIVED AT THE front desk of the MRO to see Irvin manning the phones today. She wasn't well acquainted with the Tracker, but he was nice enough. He'd been placed in the office when his Hunter passed away on a mission and he hadn't found a new partner yet. His caramel-coloured hair was styled neatly and he smiled warmly as Sera approached.

"Good morning, Tracker Seraphina, how can I help you today?"

"Hi, Tracker Irvin, I'm wanting to see my father in the infirmary, please."

He looked puzzled. "Your father? That's Tracker Allen, right? I didn't realise he was in the infirmary, what happened?" he asked as he picked up the phone and dialled the internal number for the medic team.

"He's been unwell for a couple of days and checked in last night." She waited while he spoke quietly. Sera plucked at a loose thread on her shirt and shifted her weight impatiently.

Hanging up, he said with a frown, "He's not there, Tracker Seraphina."

"Really? I thought he'd be finished up with the medical tests by now."

"No, I mean, he was never there. Who told you he was in the infirmary?"

"What?" she exclaimed. "I called the after-hours line last night and early this morning and spoke to Quill who said he was here! He was asleep when I called last night and then getting tests done with the medical team this morning so I didn't get to speak to him directly…" She trailed off, fear lancing her heart, her breathing erratic and a strange ringing in her ears.

"Quill? There is no Quill who works here. Trust me, I know everyone who works behind the desk. I've never heard of a Quill."

"What in the Four Gods' name has happened then?" she cried. Irvin watched sympathetically as she pulled her phone out and called her father. The phone went straight to his voicemail once more. Hanging up, she blinked the tears out of her eyes. "Can you please contact Tracker Helena and let her know my father is missing?" she asked around the lump in her throat. "I've got to go."

Leaving the MRO behind, she flew along the pavement, sprinting to the stables. Pushing her fears aside, she reached out to Arius.

I'm sorry to keep doing this but I need your help again.

Are you all right, my love?

My father was never at the infirmary. He's gone missing. I have no idea where he is, or if he's even… she was unable to complete the sentence, refusing to believe that he was dead.

I'll do a scout for you and see what I can find. Link your mind to me later tonight and I'll let you know if I've found anything.

Thank you. I love you, Arius.

A warm rumble filled her head. *I love you too, Seraphina. Stay safe, my love.*

Fly fierce.

Strike strong, he responded.

She'd arrived at the stables now so cut off her connection with her Soulbound. Entering the well-kept barn, she rushed down the line of stalls that opened into the paddocks. Locating Balthazar's, she peeked over the stall door. The buckskin unicorn was lying down, snoring softly. A small sliver of guilt pecked at her for waking him, but this was an emergency.

"Balthazar," she called softly.

With a grunt, he woke up and looked around in a daze. Spotting her head over the door, he nickered softly and stood up. "Seraphina." His deep voice was a welcome sound after not seeing him for three days.

"How are you?" she asked as she let herself in and wrapped her arms around his neck, burying her face in his black mane.

He tucked his head over her shoulder and pulled her close, whuffling into her auburn hair. "I'm much recovered, thank you. Not quite at full strength, but I should be well enough to return to work next week."

"That's so good to hear, I've been worried about you." She kept her face hidden, struggling to control the panic that threatened to overwhelm her.

"Something is wrong. What's happened, Seraphina?"

"A lot," she mumbled, her voice cracking. "I don't have time to explain everything right now, but I wanted to let you know that Dad's gone missing."

Balthazar pinned his ears back and asked, "What? How? What can I do to help?"

She explained how she'd gone to see him after he'd gotten sick and found his apartment broken into. She shared her theory on how someone named Quill must have hacked into the MRO's phone system and lied to her. She added, "I don't want you hurting yourself on my account, especially since you're not fully recovered, but if I could ask you to keep an ear out and do what you can with your magic to help me track him or figure out who Quill is, I would be forever grateful."

"Of course. I will do everything in my power. I have great respect for Tracker Allen."

"Thank you, Balthazar. I have to go now but I'm so glad you're feeling better." She kissed his whiskery muzzle, opened the stall door and left. As the sun reached its peak, she wandered through the city and pondered on the baffling disappearance of her father. Wrestling her emotions into submission, she strove to remain detached and considered the events analytically as if it were one of her tracking assignments. Now that she thought about it, it was almost certain that he'd been hurt or abducted when his apartment was broken into. Considering there was no blood and no body, she assumed he'd been taken.

But why? What purpose does he serve? And who is Quill and why would he lie to me?

A lightbulb went off in her brain and she knew the answer as surely as she knew she was bound to Arius.

President Kaesus is behind this.

She wasn't sure why he was targeting her family but she had a hunch he would use Allen against her. Resolve hardening, she vowed to destroy the President however she could. Hatred for the man who had wiped her memories and now abducted her father burned within her.

I can't do anything to save Dad for the moment, but I can make life difficult for the President by stealing the IRC plans for the Little Birds.

Mind made up, she headed for Tregua Park. As she walked, Sera wondered whether to call Hazel to bring her up to speed. After a short internal debate, she decided against it. She wanted to keep Hazel as safe as possible, and sharing her theory of abduction by their President and involving her in a top-secret mission would definitely put her life at risk. On the way, she bought two ham and cheese sandwiches from one of the cafes on Main Street: one for her and one for Wren. Striding across the lawn, she made a beeline for the welcome shade of the Peace Tree. Once she stood beneath its flowering boughs, Sera whistled to Wren. A few moments later, he dropped from the branches and crouched, catlike, in front of her. She tossed him the second sandwich wrapped in brown paper and he caught it easily, wolfing it down immediately.

"I have a message for the Little Birds. Can you pass it onto them for me, please?" she asked.

"Yep," he mumbled around his mouthful.

"Please tell them, I accept their task. If anything happens to me before I get the plans to them, tell them to find my PSB and it will give them everything they need."

The skinny boy nodded solemnly and said, "I'll go to them tonight. And Miss Sera," he hesitated, blushing, before muttering bashfully, "thank you for your gifts." He leapt back into the tree before she had a chance to respond.

She smiled to herself and whispered, "You're welcome, Wren."

CHAPTER TWENTY-FIVE

STRIDING AWAY FROM THE orphan boy's hideout, Sera reached out to Arius. Their mental link seemed to be growing stronger as she connected to him with ease at larger distances.

What a day. Can we meet?

Of course, Seraphina. I'm just in the forest to the south of Mandar City but I will come to you now.

Can I come to you? I don't think it would be safe for me to stay at home.

That might be a good idea after what I've found out. I believe your father may be imprisoned in the Iniques Rehabilitation Centre. I took note of his scent at his apartment and followed his trail. It led me to a hidden entrance just outside the fence of that prison.

Huh. I had my suspicions that President Kaesus abducted him and I suppose it makes sense for him to imprison him there.

Your instinct was right. Approval radiated through his tone. *Even though it's a terrible situation, you sound... determined. Has something happened?*

Yes. This morning I met with a group called the Little Birds. They have asked me to steal the blueprints for the IRC so they can rescue one of their members. Now I can ask them to rescue Dad, too. Sera continued walking along the pavement and sensed a vague tugging in her chest, leading her south as she focused on finding Arius.

Goodness. Surprise and worry laced his voice. *You have been busy. It sounds dangerous. Have you really thought this through?*

Yes. I appreciate your concern, but I don't need you to shield me from every possible threat. President Kaesus needs to pay for everything he's done. This is one way I can screw him over. Plus, the Little Birds member that they're rescuing? He's my old professor. I don't want to see him killed just because I was too scared to help.

A heavy pause punctuated their conversation and Sera started to wonder whether she'd lost their connection. Finally, Arius replied. *If it's this important to you, then I want to help. Where do you have to steal the blueprints from?*

Her heart swelled at his support. *Apparently, the only copy in Mandar City is on the President's wristband.*

Well, that could be problematic.

You're right there! However, I've had someone offer to help me from inside the MRO. We have a plan but everything hinges on tomorrow night.

What's happening tomorrow night?

It's the annual Choosing Ceremony for the graduates from MINATH. The Hunters choose their partnered Tracker and then they both choose the unicorns they will ride for their missions. All past graduates of MINATH are invited to attend. The President will be giving a speech and I'll sneak away and steal the plans whilst he's distracted.

I'll come with you. I want to help.

She paused and considered his offer. *You might be helpful as a distraction in your human form. And if everything turns to shit, then we may need to make a quick getaway through the skies.*

I can do that.

Thank you, Arius. Fatigue pulled at her limbs as she abandoned the pavement and stumbled through a ploughed paddock. *I have to go now. I'm too tired to talk and walk at the same time.*

That's perfectly fine. Go. I will see you soon.

Sera withdrew her mind and pulled her phone out, ready to text Hazel. Her finger hovered over the keypad as she contemplated how much to explain over the phone.

'I'm staying with Arius tonight. Found out some weird stuff today. Keep the door locked and don't open it for anyone.'

Her friend responded almost immediately.

'Okay, Sera. Look after yourself. I'm sorry, I didn't make it over to see your Dad this morning, but I can go to the infirmary now if you need me to?'

'Don't go there. I won't go into it over text, but he's in danger, and not just from his illness.'

'Oh my gosh, Sera! That sounds horrible! Is there anything I can do to help?'

'No, I don't want to risk putting you in the line of fire too.'

'I can handle myself. Tell me if there's any way I can help. With everything going on, will I still see you at the Choosing tomorrow night?'

'Yes, I'll be there.'

'Do you have something to wear for the ceremony?'

'Shoot. I'd forgotten it's black-tie. Not really, but I'll just wear my old black dress. Hopefully no one will be paying me any attention.'

'I've got a spare dress you can wear. I'll hang it in your room before I leave. I'll be heading over early to finalise some last-minute arrangements. Take care. xx'

'Thanks, Hazel. You're a champion. You too. See you tomorrow night. xo'

As the sun sunk towards the distant mountains in the west, Sera entered the forest, her world plunging into shadows beneath the thick canopy. As she walked further into the wilds, the gloom deepened as the new moon greeted the stars above Mandar. With no moonlight to guide her way, she turned on her phone's torch to avoid tripping on the uneven ground. The curious tugging sensation in her chest kept steering her south. The general hum of the night-time creatures kept her company on her trek. When the crickets hushed their chirping unexpectedly, Sera paused and listened. Soft footfalls were headed straight for her. Instead of reaching for Firinne, which she would have done a week ago, she opened her mind briefly and sensed the comforting aura of Arius. Grinning, she turned her torch off and hid behind a trunk. She waited until his footsteps reached the tree, then she jumped out in an attempt to scare him.

Keeping a straight face, Arius, in human form, folded his arms and raised an eyebrow. "You do realise that since we've been Soulbound I can sense where you are? It is impossible for you to surprise me."

"Damn!" she exclaimed.

He kissed her softly, his eyes crinkling in merriment as he said, "You're welcome to keep trying if you want, though. Who knows, maybe one day I'll be distracted enough for you to catch me out."

She chuckled and embraced him, laying her head against his bare chest. His heart beat slowly and warmth soaked into her.

Pushing away reluctantly, she said, "Before I forget, I have a favour to ask. If you're right that my dad is being held in the IRC and I'm successful in getting the plans tomorrow, we can't waste any time in getting him out of there. I'll let the Little Birds know so we can work together to get Tormund and Dad at the same time. But I wanted to ask, will you help me rescue him? Even though it might put your secret in jeopardy?"

"Of course," he agreed immediately.

"I want you to really think about this, Arius," she insisted. "If things go badly and you are forced to transform to save us, then you could risk exposing the existence of dragons to the world."

"I've been giving this a lot of thought since I lost you," he said slowly. "To be honest, I believe it's time for us to reveal ourselves."

"But what about what Talegar said on the plateau?"

Arius glared at the mention of his father's name. "That dragon pretends to care for the wellbeing of dragonkind, but he's really only looking out for what's best for himself. The decision shouldn't only be up to him."

"Fair enough." She held her hands up in a placating manner. "In that case, could you do me a favour? Tomorrow, do you think you could find Torvold and Idris? They offered to help and I think we'll need all the support we can get."

He bobbed his head. "I can do that for you. Now, come," he whispered. "It is time to rest."

He took her hand and led her carefully through the trees, not needing a torch to negotiate the undergrowth. She followed blindly, trusting him completely. Arriving in a clearing, he reluctantly released her hand and stepped away. Leaning his head back, his face bathed in the starlight, he released a slow exhale and transformed. Sera watched in awe as spines erupted along his back, coppery scales coated his skin and leathery wings sprouted from his shoulders. He grew until his body blocked out the stars. This was the first time she'd seen him in his true form since her memories had returned. Sera sucked in a breath as she took it all in. Her memories hadn't done him justice. He was magnificent. She could easily walk beneath him without grazing his belly. He stretched his wings and shook his head, sending ripples down his scaled hide.

"That's better," he said before meeting Sera's gaze.

His swirling emerald irises captivated her. She stepped closer, feeling the heat radiating from his skin, and caressed him. The rough texture of his scales sent a thrill through her and a tiny groan of longing escaped her lips. A comforting hum thrummed from Arius' throat and he leant his head down, pressing the tip of his snout against her body. An overwhelming explosion of joy filled her chest, enveloping her in a comforting warmth.

"I missed you," she murmured and wrapped her arms around his muzzle. "I didn't recognise that it was you I was missing, but I have been miserable since I returned home. I couldn't understand why I felt like a piece of me was lost. Now everything makes sense. I feel like... like I can face anything so long as I have you."

Without jostling her, he folded his legs and lay down, before snaking his head around her body and drawing her into his chest. "I cannot begin to tell you how much pain I endured during your absence. I am overjoyed to have you by my side once more. I will admit... before I found out you'd lost your memories, I did wonder whether you had chosen to abandon me." His voice was even but he refused to meet her eyes.

"I'm so sorry, Arius. I could never leave you. I wish I had been strong enough to stop the President from injecting me with... whatever that was." She shivered as a chill that had nothing to do with the night air prickled her skin.

"You do not need to apologise, my love. It wasn't your fault."

Sera pressed her lips to his scaled cheek before raising her gaze to scan the empty skies. "Do you think Desamor will find us here?" she asked.

"I'm not sure. I've been trying to locate him but it's proving more difficult than I anticipated. But do not fear. I will keep watch tonight." Arius brought his wing over top of her, creating a make-shift cave. Sera settled herself between Arius' foreleg and belly and rested her head against his body. The cool wind that had sprung up couldn't breach the cocoon he had formed, and the heat he generated was gloriously toasty. The earthy scent of burning embers accompanied by the soft whoosh of his breathing produced a soothing ambience that lulled her to sleep.

As her eyes drifted shut, she heard Arius whisper, "I swear I will never let harm come to you ever again, my Soulbound."

CHAPTER TWENTY-SIX

CALL IT WHAT YOU want, but my sixth sense is telling me something is wrong.

Sera stood in front of her door, staring at the number 113. She had spent a blissful morning reconnecting with Arius who had promised to accompany her to the Choosing. Now that she'd arrived at her apartment, she wished she'd asked him to come home with her, too. Passing her PSB over the door's control panel, there was no sound, meaning it wasn't locked. Stomach twisting, Sera kept her hand on the hilt of her blade and cast her mind into her home. The only life forms that greeted her were Perry's and the dull glow of the neighbours in the next-door apartment.

At least Hazel went to the Choosing early.

Sera pushed the door open slowly and peeked around it, half-expecting to see all her belongings strewn around the lounge in the same way it had been at her father's. She relaxed slightly when she could see nothing out of place.

Maybe I'm just being paranoid. To be fair, it wouldn't be surprising after the week I've had.

Wondering whether Hazel had simply forgotten to lock up, she shut the door behind her and moved into the lounge, searching for signs of an intruder. Perry came hurtling out of her room, yowling and spitting, and leapt into her arms.

"Woah, buddy! This isn't like you, what's wrong?" She soothed Hazel's cat and scratched behind his ears while he glared at her bedroom. He bunted her with his head and pressed his claws into her arm, before springing away and crawling to the top of Hazel's shelves. He hid up there, his tail whipping from side to side and his pupils dilated as he watched her enter the bedroom. Glancing around, Sera noticed the silky green dress hanging from her wardrobe that her friend had promised to leave out for her, but everything else appeared to be untouched. Moving around to the side of her bed, she noticed a brown strap peeking from underneath it. Dropping to her hands and knees, she discovered her backpack shoved under the bed. Dragging it out, she frowned.

How did my backpack get here? I abandoned it at Nanna's house. And all the food has been taken.

With trepidation, she unzipped it. A plain white envelope sat in the bottom. An icy chill slid through her veins. Slowly, she drew it out of her backpack and turned it over. There were no markings to indicate where it might have come from. Sera carefully slid her finger under the lip and broke the seal. A flash of blue greeted her, and she pulled an iridescent blue feather from the envelope.

That's weird. Who would send me a feather?

She admired the colour in the sunlight slanting through her window. Placing the feather carefully on her bedside table, she then pulled out the note that accompanied it. Unfolding the slip of paper, she read the typed message.

"For my little bird."

The hair on the nape of her neck raised and she dropped the note as if it had scolded her. She had no idea who it was from. One thing she did know though: never had four words struck such fear into her soul. Striving to remain rational, she picked up the note and set it down beside the feather.

It's just a feather, Sera, no need to freak out. Perhaps it's from the Little Birds? Or from Helena? Could it be a good luck charm? Or is there some meaning behind it?

She pondered her options. Her intuition told her to leave the feather behind. It was beautiful, but not knowing the source had her on edge. She grabbed the Seeing Stone and projected the image of the feather toward it, hoping it might shed some light on the sender. An image flickered over the surface of a dark cavern. Squinting her eyes, she strained to make out the details in the dim blue glow. When she found the source of the glow, realisation dawned. The bioluminescent fungi that sprawled down the walls and the peculiar stream that flowed upwards could only belong to the cavern that housed the Seeing Pool. The surface of the water showed the familiar image of her mother and the shadowy figure named Mal. It was a surreal feeling watching a vision within a vision. Sera could see her mother's mouth moving, but the Seeing Stone didn't have the same power as the Seeing Pool and no sound came from it. Cocking her head, she tried to recollect exactly what she'd heard that day. She'd been so excited to hear her mother's voice and worried about the dragons fighting in the cave she'd fled from that she couldn't remember the exact details of their conversation.

I know Mum said she'd had a premonition about me. Mal was upset about it. But why is the Seeing Stone showing me this again?

She clamped down on the twist in her heart at the reminder that Allen might not be her biological father. If she was honest with herself, she'd been ignoring that part of her restored memories.

Allen is my father. Even if he isn't biologically, he raised me on his own, taught me everything I know about tracking and has always been there for me. Mal has never existed in my world. That man is no father of mine. Eyeing the Seeing Stone distrustfully, she contemplated the vision. *Is it suggesting that Mal sent me the feather? How could he have learnt where I live? Or is the Stone trying to tell me something else, unrelated to the feather?*

Rubbing her hands over her face, she let out an angry huff. Glaring at the note, she stalked away to the bathroom for a shower.

Sera flattened the front of her dress nervously, uncomfortable in the beautiful gown. Taking care not to trip over her heels, she headed towards the MRO. She caught a glimpse of her reflection in a storefront window and paused, actually looking at herself. The sweetheart neckline and bejewelled emerald bodice hugged her frame before the long satin skirt fell from her waist. She'd pulled her auburn hair up into a bun, but a few tendrils had escaped to caress her neck. She begrudgingly admitted that she looked quite nice, although she couldn't wait to be back in her boots.

Whoever invented high heels deserves to be stung by a scorpius.

Interrupting her grumbling, a man in a tuxedo strode towards her. When a streetlight captured his face for a moment, she realised it was Arius. The suit accentuated his lean yet muscular body and his chocolate-coloured hair was pulled back in a low ponytail.

"Where in Ghaia's name did you get a suit from?" she called, her voice bubbling with barely repressed laughter at the expression on his face. He looked as uncomfortable as she felt.

"I have my ways," he chuckled with a wink before sweeping her into his arms. "Gods, but you look divine. You are Ghaia incarnate," he breathed, his hushed tone brushing over her lips as softly as a butterfly's wing, sending a fever racing over her skin. She blushed at his compliment and wriggled out of his grip.

"Don't forget, we have a job to do tonight. No getting distracted," she reprimanded him sternly before bursting into giggles. "Sorry," she gasped between breaths. "It's just, I've never seen you this way. You're very... handsome," she finished lamely. "Plus, I'm quietly trying not to panic."

He squeezed her shoulder before threading her arm through his and escorting her to the Choosing. "I understand. I believe in your plan and I trust your abilities. We will save your father."

Sobered by the reminder of the reason why she had committed to this scheme in the first place, she raised her chin and took a steadying breath. He kissed her cheek tenderly. "Thank you for your support, Arius. It means the world to me."

"Speaking of support, I found Idris and Tor. I've explained ev've agreed to meet us tomorrow afternoon at our clearing to discuss the plan to rescue Allen."

"That's great! I'm glad you found them."

"They are eager to assist. Tor, especially," he added with an eye roll.

She chuckled, imagining the flirtatious hippogryph's enthusiasm. With a shake of her head to refocus, they entered the MRO. A heavy feeling sat in her gut with the knowledge that everything was about to change. Briefly touching her PSB at the terminal to sign in, she guided Arius down the hall. They took a brief detour so she could place Firinne and her pistol into her locker before they exited the main building.

Sera gasped when they entered the training yard. Hazel and her committee had outdone themselves. All the equipment and training dummies had been removed and now an enormous marquee covered the entire yard. As they entered the pavilion, Sera's eyes widened as she took in the decorations. Lush cream curtains draped around the edges of the room while thousands of lights twinkled overhead. Four coloured banners hung on the far wall with the symbols for each unit: an arrow on the red banner for Hunters, a leaf on green for Trackers, a circle on blue for Negotiators and a cross on white for Alchemists. A stage had been erected in front of the banners and a microphone sat atop the podium. Lines of chairs filled the area in front of the stage for the graduates whilst small tables littered the back of the room with charcuterie boards overflowing their tops. Sera ogled the variety of cheeses and fruits displayed on the platters.

A large space beside the stage had been cleared for the unpaired unicorns to gather, ready to be chosen at the end of the ceremony. A string quartet from Harongar Isle played in the corner near them, the lilting music of the foreign instruments providing a bewitching atmosphere. It was a rare treat to hear live music, since any career in the arts was discouraged after the Mythic War while Mandar's focus was directed to survival and fostering peace. Sera stayed glued to Arius' side, trying hard to appear relaxed as other guests arrived. They mingled amongst the old MINATH graduates whilst they waited for the Choosing to begin.

CHAPTER TWENTY-SEVEN

"SERA!" HAZEL'S VOICE RANG out across the floor as she extracted herself from a spirited conversation between a unicorn and one of the graduates. "You made it! And you brought Arius." Her face fell slightly but she quickly hitched her dazzling smile back into place. Sucking in a breath, she breathed, "I knew that dress would suit you. You look amazing. And you look very smart, Arius," she tacked on.

"Thank you so much for lending it to me, Hazel. You look lovely, as well."

The gold chiffon dress swirled around her ankles as Hazel twirled, her dark tresses flowing down her back like a mane. Her glasses accented her bold eyeliner.

"I can't stay and chat, sorry. I've got to go make sure the President has arrived safely and then help get the graduates seated. Chat later!" She hurried off in a flurry of fabric. A waiter sauntered past with a tray of flutes and paused, offering them one each. They both accepted a glass and Sera took a sip, hoping the sparkling white wine might soothe her nerves a little.

Not too much though, I've got to stay sharp for the mission.

Arius swirled the drink and sniffed it dubiously, shooting a perplexed look at Sera.

She laughed and said, "It's fine, it's just wine. Although," she added as an afterthought, "if you haven't had it before, don't drink too much. It can make you a bit silly."

Glaring at the glass, he muttered, "Dragons don't get silly." He took a sip. Screwing his nose up, he looked at her incredulously. "You actually enjoy this?" He placed the drink down on the closest table before turning to her and cupping his hand behind her neck, pulling her in. His mouth was on hers in a flash and she sank into his embrace. His lips tasted like the sweet wine he had sampled, and Sera groaned quietly as they moved sensually against hers.

Leaning away, she chuckled breathlessly and asked, "What was I saying?"

"Just how I taste better than any drink you've ever tried," he said, before capturing one of the tendrils of hair that had snaked its way out of her bun and tucking it behind her ear.

"Whilst that is true, I do need to warn you; Tyler will be here tonight. If he sees you with me, he will probably be... unpleasant."

"Remind me, who is this Tyler?"

"My paired Hunter," Sera muttered. She hadn't mentioned her history with Tyler to Arius. Even though her Soulbound always seemed in control of his emotions, she wasn't sure how Arius would react if he knew how much Tyler harassed her.

Arius smirked. "I'm sure he won't be a problem."

"He's an asshole. Don't say I didn't warn you," she said as she shrugged. Tugging Arius out of earshot of their neighbours, she whispered, "I need to blend in until the President gives his speech, then I'll sneak away. I'll connect with you if I need help, but in the meantime I'll need you to cover for me if anyone asks where I've gone."

"What do you want me to say?" His dark eyebrows furrowed together.

"Um, just say I've gone to the bathroom or something."

"Why would you go to the bathroom in the middle of the President's speech? That seems a little preposterous."

She stared at him blandly. "I would be going there to do my business."

He still looked at her quizzically, not understanding. "What business?"

"I'd be going to pee!" she exclaimed, then blushed at the amused look a nearby Negotiator shot at her.

"I see." Arius' eyes widened as he finally understood, before muttering, "You humans need to relieve your bladders far more often than necessary."

She raised her eyes to the heavens and gently punched his arm. "Can I count on you or not?"

"Fine. If anyone asks, I'll say you had to use the bathroom," he grumbled.

"Thank you." She snorted and turned to grab a strawberry from a nearby platter, nearly bumping into Helena. "Thank goodness!" Sera exclaimed. "I've been wanting to speak to you. Can I trust Fra—" She cut off her sentence abruptly when she realised the Director of the MRO was accompanying the Head Tracker. The ill-natured man went by no other name other than the Director. He was middle-aged but still athletic and kept his greying hair shaved.

"Tracker Seraphina," the Director greeted her smoothly. She nodded respectfully to her boss. "It is good to see you looking so well after your time away from us. I was sorry to hear about your memory loss. I hope that, in time, you will remember everything that happened and be able to share what you learnt." He smiled, but his grey eyes remained cold. He smoothed the front of his immaculate grey suit with a tanned hand before scanning the crowd.

Helena kept a wary eye on the Director and, when she was sure he wasn't looking, gave the slightest inclination of her head.

Sera remained silent but raised her eyebrows infinitesimally in acknowledgment.

Oblivious to the silent exchange the Director announced, "Tracker Helena, we must go. President Kaesus has arrived."

Together, they left to greet the President and a shiver ran down Sera's back.

It's almost time.

She located the President as he wandered through the crowd, greeting both the MINATH graduates and employees of the MRO with a benevolent smile. She hissed quietly at the sight of him and Arius squeezed her hand reassuringly. Before she could react, Tyler interrupted her line of sight. Dressed in a sharp black suit with a violent red shirt, he watched them with his arms folded.

"Who's this clown?" Tyler snorted, glowering at Arius.

Sera raised an eyebrow. Arius was the opposite of a clown. Her Soulbound straightened and returned Tyler's glare. She noticed the barest trace of fear flicker over Tyler's face before he buried the emotion.

"This is the man you told me about?" Arius questioned Sera, wrapping his arm around her shoulder protectively. She nodded. He smirked and muttered in her ear, "If I can handle my brother, I'm pretty sure I can handle this puny human."

She held her hands up in submission. "If you say so. He has a way of getting under my skin. Hopefully yours is thicker than mine."

Arius winked and said, "We both know it is."

Tyler stepped close, closing the gap between them. "What does he mean puny human? Is he a shifter of some kind? This event is only for past students and graduates of MINATH. The only mythics allowed here are the unicorns who will be chosen at the end of the ceremony. I'm going to have to ask you to leave." His tone was congenial but the ugly spark in his eye belied a rage that begged to be released.

The last thing I need is a fight between these two. And one is brewing, I can feel it.

Stepping out from under Arius' arm, she moved between the two men and, matching Tyler's tone, said, "We were allowed to bring our partners along, Tyler. He is here as my guest."

Cheeks reddening, the Hunter looked between them, blustering. "Your PARTNER?" he spat the word. He seized Sera's arm and jerked her to his side.

Arius bared his teeth and snarled, "Get your hands off her."

"She's my Tracker. I can do what I want with her. You can piss off. Or I can make you." Tyler's grip was possessive and Sera strained to get away from him.

"Sera belongs to no one but herself." Although Arius whispered, every word was thunder. "You have no claim on her. Unhand her before I lose my temper. Your body will be nothing but a charred crisp by the time I'm finished with you." Arius hissed his threat quietly but power laced every word, leaving Tyler visibly trembling. The Hunter reluctantly released her, turned on his heel and stalked away without another word. He shot one last scowl over his shoulder that was heavy with the promise of revenge.

Sera exhaled a shaking breath before rounding on her overprotective dragon. "Great, thanks very much, Arius," she said sarcastically. "I know how to handle Tyler. Now that you've shown your protectiveness I'm not sure how I'm going to work with him in the future. He was already awful to me before tonight, but I've got a feeling my job is going to get a lot worse." She rubbed her temple and blew out a frustrated huff. Arius looked at her incredulously, obviously hurt by her words. "I'm sorry if I've upset you, but those are the facts. I can't afford to think about your feelings tonight, I have to focus on my plan."

Arius expression turned steely and he lifted his chin, averting his eyes as he said frostily, "That's fine. I understand, of course. Let us stay focused on the job at hand."

Her heart twisted at his sudden coolness but before she could say anything more to smooth things over, the Director announced over the loudspeaker, "Graduates, please take your seats in preparation for the Choosing Ceremony."

A group of twenty red, blue, green and white uniforms moved towards the chairs. The herd of young unicorns filed towards the space made for them. The rest of the guests hung back around the platters at the rear of the marquee and their murmuring subsided. The musicians stopped playing then and President Kaesus strode to the podium. Much as she hated the man, Sera could admit his presence was commanding. His cerulean suit hugged his muscular frame, accenting his piercing blue eyes. His black hair was combed into a neat style while grey streaks peppered his temples. Scanning the graduates, he gave a wide smile, the picture of a kind leader.

"Welcome," he proclaimed, "to the Choosing Ceremony for the Mandar Institute for Negotiators, Alchemists, Trackers and Hunters. Thank you for joining us, it is so wonderful to see you here tonight." With that comment he captured Sera's gaze and held it, his eyes boring into hers, making her skin crawl. Eventually breaking eye contact, he continued his speech while Sera sucked in a deep breath, having forgotten to breathe.

"This is an exciting night for our graduates. It marks the culmination of four years of training to now go out into the world and protect the citizens of Mandar from those who would disrupt the peace."

As the President continued his speech, Sera whispered in Arius' ear, "I'm going to slip out now. Wish me luck!" She squeezed his hand, hoping he had forgiven her harsh words from earlier.

His brow furrowed with worry and he mouthed the words, "Be safe."

CHAPTER TWENTY-EIGHT

FEIGNING A NONCHALANCE SHE didn't feel, Sera stole away from the crowd, casually exiting the marquee, her heels clicking against the concrete. Once inside the MRO, she hurriedly kicked her shoes off and stashed them in her locker. The stilettos would slow her down and stealth was paramount for this mission. Opening the map of the MRO on her PSB, she reviewed her route. Following Frank's instructions, she ignored the elevator and crept to a hidden service door, pressing against the almost invisible crack in the wall. The door clicked and swung outwards. Glancing back down the hallway to ensure she was alone, she slipped inside. A red light in the ceiling offered a dull glow while she took stock of her surroundings. A black steel staircase led down, while exposed metal pipes lined the wall. She ran swiftly down the stairs, bunching up her dress to free her legs and taking care to soften each footfall. After descending three flights, she located the hidden door marked on her map.

Taking a moment, she cast her mind out and sighed in relief when no other auras greeted her on that level. Exiting the stairwell, she blinked in the sudden white light of the corridor and shivered as the temperature dropped. Frank's server was kept in a chilled environment to prevent him from overheating. Passing the elevator doors apprehensively, she breathed a sigh of relief to see the glowing number remained stationary at Ground Level.

Turning a corner, she entered Frank's Server Room. Soft blue light lit up the massive space and a series of sleek white hexagonal towers created an interlocking circle in the centre.

She whispered, "I'm here, Frank. Did you get the plans?"

The AI responded, "Yes, I was successful."

"Great! What do I need to do now?"

"Go into the centre of my servers and I will use an NFC to securely transfer the file to your PSB."

"Erm, what's an NFC? Do I need to do something?" Confusion coloured her tone at the technical term.

"Near Field Connection. It means I can transfer it to your PSB remotely," he explained.

She followed his orders, thankful it wasn't anything too technical. Her basic understanding of technology hadn't extended much further than writing up her Tracker reports. From her position in the middle of the ceiling-height-towers, she was unable to see the entrance to the Server Room, putting her on edge. "How long will it take for the plans to transfer over?"

"It will take less than a minute. The file was encrypted but I've managed to decrypt it for you. Once the transfer is complete, it will be saved under your Downloads. The Little Birds will be able to copy it from there onto their system easily."

"Thanks again, Frank. I can't quite believe the plan has worked. It almost feels too easy." She rubbed her arms as her skin pimpled from the cold. "All I need to do is get out of here without raising suspicion and we're golden."

"Happy to help." The robotic voice didn't sound happy, but she was growing used to his monotone.

Sera watched anxiously as the progress bar on her PSB crept toward one hundred percent. She shifted her weight between each foot as the cold penetrated her bare feet.

Finally, Frank announced, "The file has been transferred successfully."

The green progress bar on her screen flashed, "Download Complete," at the same time.

With a tap, she double-checked the file was indeed in her Downloads and grinned at the sight of the detailed IRC blueprint that filled her screen. "Amazing, thank you, Frank!" she exclaimed.

"You're welcome, Tracker Seraphina. I wish you luck on the next step of your journey."

Hurrying out of the Server Room, she rounded the corner into the hallway and froze. The glowing number beside the elevator doors was descending towards the basement.

"Frank," she hissed, "someone's coming!"

The silence that greeted her seemed to drag on forever as the lift dropped. The corridor was void of hiding spots. The only ways out were forward into the service stairwell or back into the Server Room. The elevator doors would open before she made it to the stairs, and she was reluctant to return to Frank's server where she'd be cornered. She groaned inwardly, knowing in her heart it had been too easy. Just as she was about to give up on Frank's help, a hidden door in the hallway opened beside her. Throwing herself inside the cleaner's closet, she offered a silent thank you to the AI.

As the doors slid open, Frank's voice echoed out of the elevator when he announced, "You have arrived at the Basement, housing the Server Room."

Holding her breath, she pressed her ear to the door and listened to the steps tramping down the hall, passing her hiding place. The clump of boots echoed on the polished concrete as someone entered the Server Room. Sera cracked the door and peeked out. This might be her only chance if the guard or cleaner or whoever they were decided to check the closet. There was no sign of anyone so she gathered her gown in her hand again and eased out of the closet, before bolting for the hidden entrance to the service stairwell.

As she sped up the stairs, the metal clanged, making too much noise to escape notice. She winced when a voice shouted below her. If she could make it back to the marquee and blend in she might still evade her pursuer. Her feet pounded on the stairs, the steel biting into her bare feet. She breathed a small sigh of relief when she made it to the hidden door on the Ground Level. The echo of her pursuer's steps bounced off the walls of the stairwell. Not pausing to check if anyone was in the MRO corridor, she tumbled out and threw the door closed behind her.

Dashing down the hall, she made the snap decision to forgo her heels in the locker room. Her dress was long enough to cover her feet, anyway. She was almost at the exit. Turning the corner, she ran straight into Arius. The collision knocked all the wind from her body and she doubled over, wheezing. The hidden door slammed closed behind her and the pounding footsteps drew near.

Face fierce with concern, Arius whispered, "Do you need me to engage them in physical combat?"

"Not yet, let's try something first," she panted. "If my idea doesn't work, then sure, take him out."

She grabbed Arius' hair and pulled him close to her, drawing his lips to hers. He moaned and pushed her against the wall, spreading his fingers over her hips.

The guard rounded the corner and drew up short, bewildered. "Did you see someone run past here?" he demanded gruffly.

"We were a little distracted." She giggled breathlessly. "But I think I heard someone head that way." She extracted one hand from Arius' locks and pointed towards the MRO's entrance, away from the Choosing Ceremony.

The guard hesitated and looked between them and the long corridor leading toward the front desk. Sera could almost see the gears ticking over in his head as he worked out that it would be nearly impossible for someone to have disappeared that quickly. Arius obviously realised the same thing and his muscles tensed, ready to fight. The guard turned back to them and opened his mouth to interrogate her when a brilliant flash of light from outside the doors, followed by a massive tremor, shook the building. With a yell, the guard grabbed hold of the wall to steady himself.

"What in the Four Gods' name was that?" Sera exclaimed.

Arius grabbed her hand and they ran out into the training yard. They stared in shock at the sight that greeted them. Lightning had struck the marquee, setting it alight. Most of the humans and unicorns were running towards Arius and Sera to escape into the relative safety of the building. Some of the unicorns were using their magic to attempt to extinguish the fire, but the flames had taken hold. Thunder continued rolling overhead as more lightning forked across the sky. Thick droplets of rain spattered the scene but did nothing to quell the blaze.

"No!" Arius cried and looked at Sera, pain filling his gaze. "Desamor is here. It looks as if dragons will be revealed tonight, whether my father wills it or not." He crushed his lips to hers and said hoarsely, "I love you, Seraphina. Don't ever forget that."

Then he transformed.

CHAPTER TWENTY-NINE

SCREAMS FILLED THE YARD as Arius returned to his true form. Sera watched in awe as the monstrous copper dragon took the place of the man beside her. He roared his challenge to his brother before taking off. His powerful wingbeats whipped Sera's dress around her legs before sending the burning marquee tumbling to the ground. He spewed forth a torrent of fire into the night, lighting the sky up. It revealed a dark shape cloaked in the thunderclouds, and Desamor snarled his returning challenge. Sera squinted anxiously through the pouring rain as Arius joined his brother. Their massive wings beat the air as they hovered, sizing each other up.

"Desamor!" Arius bellowed. "Leave this place. Your fight is not with the humans."

"That's where you're wrong, dear brother," returned Desamor. "Humans are the reason our mother is dead! They are the reason dragons have been forced into hiding for decades. We are the ultimate predator. It is they who should be hiding from us! It is time the balance of power was corrected."

"It's not that simple," implored Arius. "I appreciate that it hurt all of us deeply to lose Mother, but the humans lost loved ones because of us as well. Don't punish these humans who had nothing to do with our loss."

Desamor roared, refusing to engage in rational dialogue. "You still stand up for them? I suppose I shouldn't expect anything more from a lover of those two-legged fleshsacks," he spat. "You have betrayed our family! You have betrayed what it means to be dragonkind. You are no dragon. You are weak. And you need to be put down."

Arius growled at Desamor's tirade. "Please, Desamor, leave. This is the last time I will ask. I don't want to hurt you."

The black dragon laughed wickedly. "It's not I who will be hurt, Arius. Good-bye, brother."

Desamor dove forwards, mouth wide. Sera stared in horror as the two dragons locked together, snapping at each other's throats. Dropping her gaze, she realised President Kaesus had remained in the yard and was watching her with an evil smile. Torn between the insistent need to help her Soulbound and exacting revenge on the man who had stolen her memories and possibly her father, she settled on flipping him the bird. As childish as it was, it gave her a thrill of satisfaction when his eyebrows raised in indignation.

Abandoning her vengeful plans for now, she dashed inside to the locker room and grabbed her pistol and Firinne. Racing down the hall, she ignored the chaos of screaming graduates and mashed the elevator's button. As soon as the doors opened, she leapt in and smacked the number for the Hunter's Hub. Once the lift's doors slid closed, she entered Arius' mind. She flinched at his pain from the wounds already inflicted by Desamor.

I'm here for you, Arius. Can I offer you my strength?

Save it for later, he bit out, keeping his focus on the fight. *I'm managing for the moment.*

She buried herself in the back of his mind as she exited the lift onto the fourth floor so she could keep an eye on what was happening without distracting him. Heading straight to the external door, she deserted the safety of the Hunter's Hub and ran outside onto the balcony. Rain poured down and lightning crackled overhead. Scanning the skies, she quickly located the battling dragons. They were flying directly towards Sera. She raised her pistol and took aim. Flaring his wings, Arius adjusted his trajectory and flew over her, clearing the building easily.

Desamor followed him closely, but his more muscular frame meant he didn't have the same agility as his younger brother. As his chest smashed into the roof of the MRO, she emptied her entire magazine into his belly. The bullets didn't even mark his scaled armour. He thundered his fury before pushing off with his talons, sending chunks of concrete and glass shattering toward the ground. Sera hurled herself against the building to avoid the worst of the debris that crumbled overhead.

Sensing Arius' concern for her welfare, she strengthened her mental connection to him. *I'm fine. I'm coming to help. I won't let you fight alone.*

I wish you wouldn't, he said, but he sounded exhausted already. The time he'd spent in human form at the Choosing had sapped his energy.

The building had stopped collapsing so Sera cautiously stepped out of her hiding place. Keeping an eye trained above to watch for more falling rubble, she located the ladder that ran from the fourth-floor balcony to the roof. The metal rungs were slick from the rain and her green dress was sticking to Sera's thighs. With a sad sigh and an internal apology to Hazel, she used Firinne to slice the bulk of the skirt off. As she carefully climbed the ladder, the roars of the battling dragons echoed over Mandar City. Once on the roof of the MRO, she looked out over the city, while the wind tore at her clothes and the rain soaked into her skin.

Avoiding a high-rise, Desamor flew straight at Arius, bellowing his rage. He spread his wings wide and swung his legs forward, talons extended. Arius barrel rolled at the last second, swinging his tail as he twisted away, and grinned grimly as it connected with his brother's body. The black dragon screamed his fury and banked swiftly, coming at Arius again, catching him by surprise.

The two dragons smashed together, the collision an explosion of sound. They scrabbled at each other's underbelly with their claws, while their massive heads snapped at whatever was within reach. Desamor clamped his jaw on his brother's foreleg and Arius screeched in pain. Arius swung his head around and managed to lock his teeth onto Desamor's neck. The city lights danced over their copper and obsidian scales as they waged war between the buildings. Thick red blood streamed off them both as the thunder rolled above, echoing through the streets. Desamor spewed fire at Arius but instead burnt a nearby high-rise. The apartment tower's concrete façade began to melt from the dragon fire.

Mythics and humans stood frozen, faces upturned as they stared in disbelief at the epic battle playing out above them. The dragons tumbled through the air, plummeting towards the ground. The onlookers screamed and ran for cover. Breaking apart at the last second, they beat their wings fiercely to remain airborne. This was the moment she'd been waiting for. Even though fear had stopped her from entering the third level of a dragon's mind since her memories had returned, she had to push past that now.

For Arius.

Taking a deep breath, Sera closed her eyes. Running her trembling fingertips over Firinne's staghorn handle, she sank into her meditative state.

She ignored the storm.

She released her mental link to Arius.

She let go of her fear.

And she delved into Desamor's mind.

It had changed. Desamor's mind had grown into a twisted, sickly thing since the last time she'd connected with him. On the first level where she'd normally create the mental link to speak with him, only a dull roaring met her. No words or barricades resisted her presence. Imagining herself as a wraith, she moved through it easily. As she entered the second level, oily tendrils of madness snaked towards her. They had coiled around his memories, squeezing the joy from them, until all that remained was pain. A pang of pity seized Sera's heart.

No wonder Desamor can't be reasoned with. His mind is broken. But I can't afford to expend my energy on sympathy when his only thought is to kill Arius.

Even the searing pain of his injuries seemed to be muffled. Shoving through the frenetic images of his past, she pushed on towards the glowing green door of the third level. She allowed the discordant ocean of his thoughts to propel her forward and her consciousness crashed into it, shattering the fragile door off its hinges.

Shit. That can't be good.

Everything went quiet. Desamor's mind stilled and he hung suspended in the air for a moment. Then his nose dipped toward the ground and he dropped from the sky. Sera frantically gathered the green lines that controlled his body and manipulated them like he was her puppet. A sickening feeling settled in her bones as she manually beat his wings and navigated Desamor's body towards the ground. She sensed then that she had done irreparable damage to his consciousness.

At least Arius and Mandar City are safe.

The thought didn't make her feel any better about what she'd done. Landing him on the road in front of the MRO, she gently laid his head down and withdrew her consciousness. Coming back to her own mind, she heaved, bringing up the wine and strawberries from the Choosing. Looking through her own eyes, she stared down in horror at the still form of Desamor. Clammy and horrified, she sank to her knees. As the rain abated, Arius landed heavily on the roof behind her.

"What have I done?" she whimpered.

"What you had to do," Arius stated calmly.

"Oh, Arius!" she cried. "I'm so sorry. He'd gone mad but when I took over control, it's as if his mind snapped. I don't think he can come back from that. I didn't know how else to save you."

"It's all right, my love," he comforted her. "Come, let us go to him."

She climbed weakly onto his back, sitting between two spines, and he flew them to Desamor's side. The black dragon was unconscious and his breathing was even, but when Sera tried to enter his mind only a blank void remained.

Laying her hand against Desamor's obsidian cheek, she whispered, "I'm sorry I failed you. This wasn't supposed to happen."

Arius touched his nose to his brother's forehead and closed his eyes. "He wasn't always this way. He was a good big brother before Mother passed on. But since the War, his mind slowly warped until his version of reality became a twisted mess." Arius sighed heavily.

Sera looked up at her Soulbound but yelped when she realised his blood was spattering onto the pavement, hissing as it hit the ground. "You're hurt! Let me help you!"

"No. You've already spent too much energy. I will heal. At least it's all over now. And you are safe." On trembling legs, Arius leant his snout into Sera's chest. Her heart nearly burst at the contact and knowing that he had survived the terrible battle.

Thinking out loud, she murmured, "Since you helped save the city from your brother, perhaps we will have the support of the people. Maybe they will rejoice that dragonkind isn't extinct after all?"

He chuckled at her optimism. "We can only hope."

She kissed a scale on the tip of his nose and smiled, pouring all her love into the look she gave him. In the next second a massive arrow shot into Arius' shoulder. He trumpeted his pain and swung his head, tearing the projectile out of his flesh. Flaring his wings, he turned to face the helicopter that hovered between the buildings and reared up, ready to launch. As his wings took the first beat down to lift his great body into the air, his eyes widened and his legs gave out.

Time slowed down and all the sounds of the night were muffled in Sera's ears. The pavement trembled as he fell to the ground, smashing the glass windows in the MRO. Sera's soul howled as he toppled; the tearing, ripping feeling working its way up to claw out from her throat in the form of a scream. Racing to his fallen form, she ran her hands desperately over his face. His eyes rolled back in his head and only a sliver of green was visible under his slitted lid. When he didn't respond to her cries, Sera began pummelling his cheek. An insistent tug on the back of her dress broke her trance and she rounded on the person, ready to punch. It was Wren. His tiny frame shook and his dark eyes were wide with fear.

"Please, Miss Sera. We have to go."

"I won't leave him," she snapped.

"If you don't hide now, they'll take you too," he whimpered.

"Who?" she demanded. He pointed up. Two more helicopters had joined the one that had shot Arius. They were aiming another projectile at him. This time it was an electric net. She'd read about them at MINATH but had never seen one used on a mythic before. "Shit," she cursed loudly.

Wren hauled on her dress again. "Please. Come with me."

There's nothing you can do for him now. You can't rescue him if you're locked up too. Or dead.

With an animalistic cry, she tore herself away from her Soulbound and raced after Wren to a nearby laneway, where he pulled open a manhole. He disappeared into the sewers and, with one last anguished look back to Arius she dropped into the underground tunnel. A high-pitched keening reached Sera's ears and it took a moment for her to realise it came from her. Wrapping her arms around her middle, she sank to the ground as she listened to the tell-tale zap of the net hitting its target and the rumble of the helicopters as Arius was lifted into the air.

CHAPTER THIRTY

THE BLACK-HAIRED BOY LED the way through the maze of tunnels that made up the sewers. A strange detachment had enveloped Sera, leaving her numb. It made the pain easier to bear. All the fight in her had drained away with the capture of Arius. The only thing that kept her going was the fact that their bond told her he was still alive. When Wren reached the final bird, he whistled his signature three-note tune before clambering up the rungs. The metal covering was opened from above and Wren scrambled through the hole. Voices murmured above as Wren explained to Constantine what had happened whilst Sera hauled herself up the ladder. With the last of her energy, she dragged herself onto the dirt floor of the small room. She lay prone on the earthen floor, unable to summon the motivation to rise.

"Come on, Seraphina," murmured the werewolf, his wet nose nudging her ear. "I'll help you walk to Urma, but you've got to stand up."

With a groan, she pushed herself up. Leaning on the wolf's shoulder she staggered slowly into the Little Bird's nest. The sphinx was speaking with a snow foxen at a nearby table but turned sharply when she heard Sera's footsteps.

"Were you successful? Did you obtain the plans?" the leader of the Little Birds demanded as she padded towards Sera.

Summoning the strength to speak was difficult, but she managed to mumble out an affirmative.

"Well done!" she crowed. Urma snaked her lion's tail around Sera's shoulders and pulled her upright. "Fantastic work." Raising her head proudly, she addressed the Little Birds who were gathering around the small group. "Our newest fledgling has completed her initiation. We have the plans for the IRC. We can now start planning our extraction of Skystar. That's Tormund's codename," she added as an aside to Sera. "Come, let's get those plans downloaded." She helped Sera over to a desk and sat her down in front of a monitor. Robotically, Sera opened the Downloads folder on the screen of her PSB and initiated the transfer. While they waited for the file to download onto the Little Birds' system, Urma asked, "So, tell me, what happened? Your mission was a success, yet you appear to be dispirited?"

"My Soulbound..." she whispered and squeezed her eyes shut as the tears threatened to spill onto her cheeks. She felt herself spiralling into the pits of despair, similar to the feeling she'd had when she'd lost her memories. But this time, she knew exactly what she'd lost. As she wallowed in self-pity, a small voice disrupted her dark thoughts.

"Her dragon was captured," Wren said and slipped his small hand into hers. A tiny bubble of warmth lit up her insides at his unexpected show of affection. A glimmer of resilience peeked through the curtain of misery that clouded her mind.

You can't keep crying. Arius needs you. You've got to stay strong and save him.

Urma snorted and pronounced dismissively, "Dragons haven't been seen in Mandar City for decades."

Wren folded his arms and glared at the sphinx. "I'm not lying."

"I'm not saying you are," soothed Urma. "I'm just saying that, maybe, it's possible you simply saw a large gluxxor?"

A sudden need to stand up for the boy rose inside Sera and she met the sphinx's eyes with a scowl. "You would do well not to discount Wren's observations. Last time we met, you told me you knew that dragons still existed, yet you refuse to believe the kid when he says he saw one? The dragon he saw tonight is my Soulbound. He saved Mandar City from destruction by a second dragon bent on revenge. Now he's been captured, and I assume he's been taken to the IRC since there's nowhere else in this country that would have a hope of containing him once he wakes up."

The sphinx gawked at her, wide-eyed. "Well now, aren't you full of surprises."

Sera stood up. "They've taken my father too. I'm going with your team to the IRC and we will rescue them all."

Urma chuckled softly. "I understand your concern for the safety of your loved ones. Truly, I do. It is admirable that you wish to race into the heart of the enemy and save them. But we need to slow down and make a strategic plan. If we rush in there, guns blazing, we'll all end up dead, the Little Birds will cease to exist, and mythics throughout our country will continue to suffer under the unjust rule of President Kaesus. Give us a few days to review the plans and discuss our options. Lay low until Wednesday, then come back here and we'll tell you how you can help." Sera opened her mouth to argue but Urma interrupted. "Thank you for your service, Tracker Seraphina. You've done remarkably well. The Little Birds are thrilled to accept you into our nest." She took her leave with a curt flick of her tail, the stumps where her wings used to be catching the fluorescent light as she stalked away.

With the file transfer complete, Sera left the desk and tramped to the sewer entrance. It wasn't until she threw open the metal lid that she realised Wren had followed her.

"You can't come with me," she said gently to the young boy.

He crossed his arms and stuck out his lip petulantly. "I want to. You helped me with that angry baker months ago. It's my turn to help you."

"No. I need to be alone. I've got to figure out my next step and I can't be worrying about keeping you safe."

Wren shot a glance over his shoulder and whispered, "You're not going to listen to Urma, are you?"

She bit her lip and didn't answer.

"I won't say anything," he insisted. "I'm small and really good at hiding. I can help you."

"I appreciate the offer, Wren, but this is not a job you can help me with. I'm sorry." Sera squeezed his shoulder before climbing down the ladder. She travelled through the now-familiar tunnels, and while she trudged through the dark sewer tried to connect to Arius. Her mind hit a wall. Pressing against the barrier with her consciousness, she found no weak place to break through to her Soulbound. Their connection had been blocked.

CHAPTER THIRTY-ONE

SERA HAD PLANNED ON sneaking in to her bedroom, changing into more comfortable clothes and filling her backpack with supplies. Preferably without waking Hazel. But as she slipped silently into the apartment she yelped when the lights flicked on. Hazel greeted her from the lounge with a scathing glare and arms folded, her eyeliner smudged and her dark hair a mess of curls.

"What in Ghaia's name was that, Sera? You didn't think to mention that Arius is a freaking dragon?" she shrieked, her voice growing shriller with each word.

"Shut up, Hazel," Sera hissed, placing an urgent finger to her lips. "I don't want our neighbours to hear." Glancing at her PSB, she added quietly, "It's two am. Why are you still awake?"

"Waiting to see whether you were going to show up!"

Sera stared at her friend, surprised by her abnormally harsh tone. She didn't have time for this, but Hazel did deserve an explanation. Chewing her lip, she opened her mouth and closed it again, wondering where to begin.

"You need to start talking, Sera, right now."

"I'm sorry."

Hazel crossed her arms. "What for?"

"About your dress, for starters." Sera gestured at the tattered fabric. "And for not telling you about Arius. The thing is, it wasn't my secret to share. The dragons have been in hiding since the Mythic War. I couldn't reveal them, even to you."

"You mean there're more dragons than just Arius and that black one?"

"A lot more, by the sounds of it. I guess we'll find out soon, now that Desamor's mind is broken and Arius has been taken captive," she said bitterly.

"Oh, my gosh! I had no idea. Are you okay?" Her friend rushed to give her a hug.

Squeezing her briefly, Sera drew back and said, "I will be. I can't stay here though, Hazel. I've got to save him. And Dad. He's been abducted as well." Hazel stared at her in shock. "I refuse to put you in harm's way. They're my family and it's my fault they've been taken. I don't have time to explain everything, but the President will be after me now. I'm going to disappear for a while. I can't say where or for how long; I don't want you involved any more than you already are. I'm going to grab my backpack and get changed, then I'll get out of your hair."

Tears shimmered behind Hazel's glasses, but she swallowed hard and nodded her understanding. When Sera strode towards her bedroom, Hazel hurried to her work station and pulled tubs and vials off the shelves. Following Sera, she dumped the containers onto her bed.

"I understand why you don't want me involved but I can still help in my own way. These should be useful. I've included the usual things like Heal and Filter, plus some other treatments I've been experimenting with. They may not work properly as they haven't been tested in the field, but I've written notes on the labels, explaining what they're supposed to do. Hopefully, it helps."

Sera shot a grin at Hazel before disappearing into her ensuite to change. She called out the door, "That's perfect, thank you so much." She threaded her belt through the loops on her trousers, attaching Firinne's sheath, a small pouch and her pistol's holster as she went. Throwing on her jacket over her shirt, she swiftly deposited a canteen of water, Hazel's treatments, some dried food and the Seeing Stone into her backpack. She hesitated as she deliberated whether to take the blue feather. Throwing caution to the wind, she carefully placed it in a side pocket.

Hazel sighed and offered a sad smile. "Time for you to go, I guess. If anyone asks, I'll say I never saw you after the Choosing."

"Thanks a bunch, Hazel. I owe you big time." Sera hugged her friend and wondered how she'd ever repay her.

"Just come back safe." Her friend buried her face into her shoulder before giving her a peck on the cheek. Wiping her tears away from under her glasses, she helped Sera pull the backpack's straps over her shoulders. "Good luck, Sera," she whispered.

"Thanks again, Hazel. See you on the other side." Sera attempted a cheery wave to lighten the tension before leaving her friend alone in their home.

Sneaking out the front door of her apartment building, she dashed around the side. Keeping to the back alleys of Mandar City, Sera hugged the walls of the concrete jungle, hiding in the shadows. Unsurprisingly, there were plenty of squab patrols out tonight. Sera's mouth curled up at the memory of Wren's nickname for the IRC guards. Her smile faded when she considered whether they were only on the lookout for more dragon attacks or whether they could be hunting her. She had to utilise all of her Tracker skills to blend in and avoid detection.

When she finally made it out of the city, the sun's first rays were peeking over the horizon. Fatigue dragged at her limbs but she couldn't stop her dogged march yet. She'd been awake for twenty-four hours now and would need to rest before she launched her rescue plan. Slowly, she traipsed through the forest to the south of Mandar City until she found the clearing where she and Arius had slumbered together. The grass was trampled and furrows marred the earth where his talons had dug in. With a melancholy sigh, she sought out a comfortable spot in Arius' imprint and lay down. Before giving in to her exhaustion, she tried once more to connect to her Soulbound. The barrier remained in place, however she sensed a tugging in her chest to the north. He was almost certainly incarcerated at the Iniques Rehabilitation Centre. Mind made up to launch a rescue once she'd recovered, she relaxed into the earth. Her eyes immediately closed and she fell into a deep sleep as the rising sun painted her skin with its gentle caress.

The snorting of a nearby creature roused Sera. Jerking awake, she panicked and leapt up, eyes struggling open in the late afternoon sun, and brandished Firinne wildly. The amused expressions of Tor and Idris met her when she finally stopped stumbling around the clearing.

The lynx spoke first. "I applaud your enthusiasm for battle, but, and I mean no offence when I say this, if we had been an enemy, you'd be dead right now."

Tor sniggered but stopped short when Sera glared at him. "I mean, he's right, but we're not, so it's all good." He waggled his eyebrows in an attempt to distract her.

Scrubbing the sleep from her eyes, she mumbled, "Hi, you two."

"How are you, Sera? Arius mentioned we were meeting to plan a rescue mission for your father. Speaking of, where is Arius?" Tor asked as he looked around the clearing, puzzled by the obvious absence of the dragon.

"He's been captured," she replied grimly. Tor and Idris stared at her, aghast, as they waited for her explanation. "Desamor attacked the city last night, and Arius defended us. We managed to stop Desamor, but Arius was taken away after the battle." She couldn't bring herself to tell them how she'd broken the black dragon's mind. That story could wait for another day.

"Four Gods help us," Idris muttered in horror.

Sera continued, "I believe he's been taken to the IRC, so I need to sneak in there to rescue both him and my father. I have a copy of the IRC plans, my weapons, and my ability to sense auras, but that's about it. It will be dangerous, so I ask for your help with the understanding that you have every right to decline my request. What say you?"

The lynx and the hippogryph shared a look before Tor stepped forward and bowed his head to the ground. "You have my wings, sweet girl. Bels won't be pleased, but this is bigger than all of us. She'll get over it. Eventually."

"Bels?" Sera raised a questioning eyebrow at the mention of the bay hippogryph.

"Ah, yes, she and I have started our own flock now. I know, I know, she wore me down," he said with a wink. "I swear, I will do everything in my power to assist you in your quest to rescue Arius and your father, Sera. Should I perish on this grand adventure, make sure Bels knows of my heroic acts," he added dramatically.

Idris snorted at the hippogryph's theatrics before adding his own pledge. "I offer you my claws. When do you wish to launch your rescue mission?"

"Arius is the first dragon they've captured since the Mythic War. I'm worried about whether they will keep him alive. I can't connect with his mind, but I sense that he's still alive. For now, at least. Time is of the essence so I'm going tonight."

"Well, it sounds as if there's no time to waste, so hop aboard and let's get going!" declared Tor and knelt, allowing Sera to mount. "Race you there, cat!" He snapped his beak playfully at Idris and, as soon as Sera was securely tucked in behind his feathery wings, cantered for a few strides before leaping into the dusky sky.

CHAPTER THIRTY-TWO

A COUPLE OF KILOMETRES north-west of the Iniques Rehabilitation Centre, Sera stashed her backpack and jacket inside a hollow tree trunk in the forest. She figured it would be easier to stay undetected without a bulky pack slowing her down. Plus, if she was captured during the rescue, they wouldn't let her keep her gear anyway. It would be better left out here in case she had to make a run for it and needed food and treatments whilst hiding in the wilds. The only two ointments that she included in a pouch attached to her belt were a container of Heal and a spray bottle of Freeze. One of Hazel's creations, the label on Freeze said that if sprayed directly on the lens, it would halt the security camera's footage. Patting Firinne and her pistol, Sera ensured her weapons were secure in their sheaths. Whilst she prepared her gear, Idris sat nearby, his tail twitching in agitation, annoyed that Tor and Sera had beaten him to the meeting point.

He's crowing like an overgrown rooster that got into the grain. Idris projected his exasperated thoughts to Sera.

She chuckled. *Tor is Tor. You'll just have to get over it, I'm afraid.*

I don't need to worry about being killed in the IRC. He's going to frustrate me to death before we even get inside.

Ignoring the irritated lynx who was now baring his teeth at Tor's victory trot, she tapped her PSB and brought up the plans for the IRC to review their route.

Dragging the image of the building around to the eastern border, she spread her fingers to zoom in on the hidden entrance just outside of the IRC's fenced boundary. The forgotten doorway led into an old service tunnel that was no longer used, and the obscure exit would deposit them right inside the prison. As she studied the blueprint one last time, the screen flickered and the MRO logo of two intertwined circles replaced it.

A tinny, robotic voice cleared its throat from the small speaker on her wristband and said, "Hello, Tracker Seraphina. This is Frank. Please note, this is a pre-recorded message, I cannot hear you in real-time. When I transferred the blueprint across to your Personal Security Band, I also transferred a part of myself to assist with your mission. If you require my assistance to open a locked entry or exit, simply hold your PSB to the control panel. I should be able to remotely break the code and open the door for you."

The voice disappeared and the blueprint of the IRC returned while Sera gawked in shock. After a moment, she grinned at her companions and said, "Well, that's handy."

"Who is Frank?" asked Idris.

"He's the Artificial Intelligence that works in the Mythic Relations Office. He's the one who managed to steal the IRC blueprints from the President and transfer them to me."

"Huh. And you're sure we can trust him?" The lynx stalked close to Sera and locked eyes, his molten amber gaze piercing.

She shifted uneasily and answered hesitantly, "I think so. He's the only reason we got the plans in the first place. Plus, he hid me from a guard. At the end of the day, I don't think we have much choice. This is the only way we can get Arius and Dad out of there."

Idris inclined his head, accepting her decision. Together, the three of them slunk toward the tree line. Staying under the cover of the canopy, they circled around to the east of the IRC towards the concealed entrance. The night was warmer than expected and a hush lay over the forest, as if all the creatures watched the trio in quiet anticipation. As they travelled around the northern boundary, she kept a wary eye to her right. The entire prison was enclosed by a dome of electrified wire mesh to halt the escape of flighted mythics, and in the interior there was barbed wire fencing that sectioned off parts of the exercise yard. Sera silently thanked the Gods that only a small sliver of moon lit the sky tonight. Whilst she was pragmatic that there was a high chance of them being caught, she couldn't help firmly holding onto the belief that they'd all make it out alive.

Idris' keen nose detected the heavy metal door in the ground, even though it was covered by ferns and grass. Once they'd cleared off the worst of the undergrowth, Sera followed Frank's instructions and brought her PSB up to the control panel built-in beside the door handle. A loud click echoed through the quiet night and she smiled triumphantly.

"Frank came through with the goods!" she crowed before tugging on the handle.

The heavy door groaned as it swung open, and Idris was quick to dart behind it to help her lower it gently to the ground. A short set of metal stairs greeted them, leading to a dark, metal-plated tunnel. The three of them slipped inside and left the door open behind them. Sera immediately noticed a security camera and sprayed the lens with Freeze, praying Hazel's creation worked the way she claimed it would. Even in the darkness, she felt terribly exposed as they hurried down the underground corridor together. Her boots thumped softly against the metal floor, while Idris kept pace on silent paws and Tor's hoofbeats echoed loudly. Sera winced. She hadn't anticipated how much noise they'd make.

They made it to the other end of the tunnel without incident and she sprayed another camera before climbing to the top of the stairs. She paused and swept her consciousness out. Besides her two companions waiting behind her, she only sensed the aura of one guard nearby. He was walking away from the door in the ground. Once again, Sera held her PSB to the door and waited for the sound of Frank unlocking it. Edging it open slightly, she poked her head up and scanned the area to make sure the guard wasn't looking their way. Luck was on their side. As she watched, he rounded the corner of a nearby cell block and disappeared.

With no other guards in sight, they stealthily crept out of the concealed tunnel and shut the door behind them before sprinting fifty metres to the cover of the closest building. The IRC was made up of two buildings: a high-security cell block that stood one storey tall and sat roughly four hundred metres away from another massive multi-storey building with wings sectioned off for each category of mythic. The main building held separate branches for flighted, water-based and earth-bound mythics as well as another for humans.

From her examination of the plans, she identified the ground level of this wing as the one that housed the flighted mythics, as well as a laundry room. The plan was to get her in a clean IRC uniform to avoid questioning if they ran into other guards, then find and release Arius. Now they were here, her soul was tugging her towards the high-security cell block. They'd get his help to break out her father from the human wing and if they remained undetected, sneak out the secret tunnel. If shit hit the proverbial fan, she was relying on Arius' fire to burn through the mesh dome and fly out of here.

Closing her eyes, she focused on sweeping her consciousness through the cell block in front of her. A hundred auras assaulted her senses internally. Among the chaos of golden light, Sera managed to distinguish the human auras of the squabs. There were only a few on duty inside this part of the prison, and none near their entry. She sensed another guard walking outside the flighted mythics wing, only a few metres away from turning the corner and spying the three companions crouched by the door. Holding her PSB out to the control panel, it took a few anxious moments before the armoured door in front of them hissed open and they stole inside.

Idris' voice sounded in her head. *It seems they keep a skeleton crew for night shift. That's interesting. I expected to have to avoid more guards than this.*

You're right. I wonder why? Sera responded.

Let's hope we don't get to find out, the lynx muttered.

The prison walls were a crisp white with stark lighting. Most of the inmates appeared to be asleep on the floor behind the tempered glass of their cells. Their small rooms were padded and held no furniture. Gargoyles, harpies, hippogryphs, sphinxes and even one phoenix lay trapped in their prisons. Revulsion coiled in her gut and a fierce anger at the President made her heart pound loudly in her ears.

I wonder how many of them truly deserve to be locked up in here.

She murmured to Tor and Idris, "Stay here and keep a lookout. I'll grab a uniform and come back."

They nodded and continued examining the prisoners. Sera hurried down the hall until she reached a sliding door that automatically opened upon her approach. The room was filled with washing machines and dryers, along with rows of grey folded clothes in various sizes. She grabbed a uniform and changed in a hurry, before threading her belt into the trouser loops with her weapons attached. Shoving her own clothes into the nearest washing machine, she exited the laundry. She realised if any guard discovered them wandering the halls of the IRC she might get away with a brief inspection, but questions would be raised if they looked too closely.

At least this outfit might buy us some time.

As she scurried back towards Tor and Idris, a hippogryph in a cell on the opposite wall caught her eye. He was awake and staring at her in disbelief. He reared and beat his steel-coloured wings urgently, the tips of his feathers grazing the walls of his prison.

It was Professor Tormund.

CHAPTER THIRTY-THREE

"Tor! Idris!" she hissed. "Come here!"

Her companions immediately joined her at the cell and studied the mythic inside. Torvold gasped and jerked back. Eyes wide, he demanded, "What's he doing here?"

"Do you recognise him?" she asked.

"He's my father." He stared longingly into the cell and tapped the glass gently with his beak. "Mother banished him years ago. I haven't seen him since I was a foal. But I never forgot him." Tor's eyes glistened and he ducked his head, a shuddering breath causing his feathers to tremble.

"I don't know if this will work, but I'll give it a go." She stepped to the side of the cell and held her PSB against the control panel. Tormund watched anxiously as they waited, when a loud hiss sounded and the tempered glass lowered into the floor.

"Seraphina!" cried the grizzled hippogryph as he stepped shakily out of his cell. "What in Ghaia's name are you doing here? And who are your friends?"

Torvold interrupted Sera's response with a soft whistle.

The old professor turned his head sharply as he examined the other hippogryph. "It can't be," he whispered. Taking a step forward, his expression turned hopeful. "Torvold? My son? Is that really you?"

With a cry, Tor sprang forward and buried his face into his father's feathered shoulder. Tormund swept his wings around him and preened his son's neck.

After giving them a few moments, Sera whispered, "This is wonderful, but we really have to keep moving if we want to avoid the guards. Professor, tell us, how did you end up in the IRC?"

Together, they walked towards the exit as Tormund explained. "It seems my little speech about the existence of dragons was not appreciated by the authorities." A dark shadow crossed his face. "It turns out I was right! I heard the squabs talking earlier, the President has brought in a dragon this very day!"

"He's who we're here to rescue," Sera said. With a slight smile, she added, "We don't understand why it happened, but he and I are Soulbound." She held up her palm to the Professor, showing the golden scar.

"Four Gods! What a peculiar thing to happen! You must be distraught to have had your Soulbound captured."

She grimaced. "Yes. That's putting it mildly." As they strode down the corridor, she faltered at the cell of a male harpy. The blue-haired mythic was lying on the ground, with oxygen tubes coming from his nose and wires hooked up to a machine. Every now and then his body twitched and the veins in his pale skin appeared blue in the white light. "Professor," she began but Tormund interrupted with a smile.

"I'm no longer your teacher, Seraphina, you don't have to call me professor anymore."

"Fine, Tormund then. Why is that harpy hooked up to those wires?"

"My dear girl. Have you not yet realised what the true purpose of this place is?" he asked sorrowfully.

She shook her head, confused by his question.

"The IRC parades as a place where mythics and humans who have made the wrong choices in life have the opportunity to redeem themselves through counselling and community service. Everyone knows it acts as more of a prison than a true rehabilitation centre. However, what they really do is torture and conduct experiments on mythics. If there's a mythic who has a magical talent that the President wishes to harness as a weapon, or whose relatives he can exploit in the outside world, those poor souls are subjected to a terrible fate. It would be better to just let them die."

Sera felt her stomach roil at the revelation. All these years she had blindly accepted her government's narrative as the truth. To think that every mythic she'd helped track down might have been subjected to this torment made her question everything she'd ever known. Aloud, she murmured, "Ghaia, help us."

"Sadly, it seems the Four Gods have forsaken these mythics," Tormund declared sorrowfully.

She paused when she realised Idris was no longer padding beside her. Glancing over her shoulder, she found him motionless except for his ears flicking forward and the flames around his neck flaring in distress.

"It seems the Gods have forsaken us too. Squabs approaching from our front," he hissed, his tail whipping from side to side.

Sera cast her mind out and sensed the auras of two guards about to turn the corner into their hallway. "Shit," she cursed and shoved her wrist at the control panel. She might have been able to get away with the story of moving two prisoners by herself, but moving three on her own with no obvious restraints would immediately raise questions.

The four of them raced through the armoured door, Sera trailing behind. As the door hissed shut, she heard one of the squabs call out to them. Not taking any chances, they dashed around the corner of the flighted mythic cell block before sprinting across the exercise yard, towards the high-security prison. Slowing only to open a gate in the barbed wire fence, they continued toward the glow of the solitary building. As the two hippogryphs cantered ahead of her, their eagle eyes sweeping the area for guards, Sera noticed Idris was no longer with them.

"Stop," she commanded. Turning around, the hippogryphs cocked their heads in confusion as she scanned the area for the lynx.

"We can't stay in the open, Sera," whispered Tor.

"I know, but we can't leave Idris behind."

Idris? Can you hear me?

There was no reply from the lynx. His black coat would melt into the shadows of the night so she opened her mind to search for his aura. Before she could cast her net wide enough to locate him, she discerned a squad of guards approaching from the high-security block. She screamed a warning but it was too late. A lasso made of iron links snaked through the air and landed around Tor's neck. Many of the weapons used to subdue mythics were made of iron to quell their magical abilities. Tor reared in panic, wings flapping violently, unable to find who had thrown the metal rope. Some strange power concealed the guards from their eyes, yet Sera could still see their auras.

Through her alarm, she managed to focus enough to count them and yelled, "There are eight of them, three in front of you, Tor, and five coming for you, Professor!"

"You will not harm my son," the grizzled hippogryph screamed at the empty air. Lunging forward, his beak snagged the lasso and pulled, dragging it over Torvold's head. "Fly, son! Get away while you still can!"

"I can't leave you and Sera!" Tor argued.

"You must!" insisted Tormund.

"Save yourself, Tor." Sera added her voice to the fray. "You can't help us if you're dead!"

With a deeply pained expression, Tor leapt into the air, spinning and diving to avoid the bullets shot in his direction. Wings beating frantically he made it out of range and disappeared toward the secret tunnel. Meanwhile, Tormund had dived forward and was striking wildly in an attempt to take out as many guards as he could. Heavy thuds met his hooves as three guards lay unconscious on the ground, visible now that he'd knocked them out. The other five were converging on the old mythic as Sera raised her pistol.

One, two, three. Three shots. Three bodies. Three auras snuffed out by her hand. She shook uncontrollably as she loaded the next round of bullets.

I can't think about the three lives I have taken tonight. Not yet.

Swallowing the bile in her throat, she squeezed the trigger to take out the seventh guard. A knife sailed through the air towards her and she cried out, jerking the gun as she lurched, and missed her target. The blade was not meant for her though. Striking Tormund, it sliced easily into his chest. He paused his fierce attack and looked down at the blade. A puzzled expression flitted across his face as he watched the red blood drip from the wound. Raising his head, he caught Sera's eyes and gave a soft smile.

"Better this than ending up as one of their experiments. Tell Tor I always loved him. And then go save the world, Seraphina." Tormund's voice trailed off and he fell to his knees as the blood pooled around him. With a sigh, he closed his eyes and crumpled to the ground.

EPILOGUE

BEATEN AND DRAGGED INTO the high-security block, Sera blinked the blood out of her eyes. Her captors dropped her to the floor and exited, the door hissing closed behind her. A blurry figure stood in the centre of the hallway that stretched away from her. Squinting, Sera tried to make out the person through the blinding white light. Slowly, the features of President Kaesus came into focus.

"Good evening, Sera. What a merry time you've had, hmmm? And you were so close to saving everyone you loved... or were you?"

He raised his arm, presenting his own PSB, and pressed a button. Frank's pre-recorded message echoed in the empty space.

The President chuckled. "Oh, Seraphina. How naïve you are. AIs don't have feelings. They don't care about equality. I arranged for his coding to be altered to help you and fed him the IRC blueprints. A tracer was added to the file he gave you, so I knew exactly where you were the whole time. As a bonus, you've been particularly helpful in showing me precisely where the Little Birds' nest is, so thank you for that."

"What?" she gasped and struggled upright. Surprised to find she still had her blade, she released Firinne from its sheath.

"Now, now, let's not be too hasty," he pacified, his cordial tone at odds with the evil glint in his eye. He pulled a pistol from his belt and aimed it towards a door on his right. Two guards dragged a limp prisoner between them into the hallway. Sera moaned when she recognised the shackled man. It was Allen. With obvious effort, he raised his head and met her gaze. His face looked worse than Sera's felt. Her heart squeezed to see his pain.

"Not Dad," she whispered, loosening her grip on Firinne, afraid that any threatening movement on her part would doom Allen to more torture.

"He is not your father," the President thundered.

"What?" She turned her head sharply to stare at him. "How do you know about the vision..." Slowly, she pieced things together in her head. She whispered in horror, "Malcolm Kaesus. Your name is Malcolm. Shortened to Mal. Mal. No, no, no." She gripped her head in her hands as her world imploded. Digging her nails into her scalp, Sera desperately wanted to deny the truth. He smirked, his penetrating blue eyes razing her with their intensity. The same sapphire blue as hers. How had she not paid attention to the colour of his eyes before?

The time for playing it safe has passed. With a feral snarl, she launched herself at him, Firinne poised, ready to strike. Everything seemed to move in slow motion then. Unsurprised by her attack, Malcolm squeezed the trigger and shot Allen in the chest. Sera's heart shattered and she screamed as she watched his body jolt from the impact. The President then swung the pistol forward and shot her square in the chest. Pain like she'd never experienced before streaked through her body, as the force sent her flying backwards. Firinne flew from her grasp as she smashed into the floor and lay in a broken heap, unable to move. She took a shuddering breath as she waited for her life to end. Confusion warred against the pain when she remained conscious. Her limbs were locked but there didn't appear to be any blood.

Heavy footsteps echoed in the hall as Malcolm stalked toward her. He knelt, pressing the muzzle into her cheek, and whispered, "Sorry, sweetheart. No death for you. Not yet, anyway. There's someone I want you to meet."

Realisation dawned when she noticed the pistol in front of her was set to stun. Malcolm grabbed her by the collar and dragged her down the hall. Passing her father's prone form, she could only hope he was simply paralysed too. As they made their way past another cell door, Sera felt the familiar tug of Arius' soul. Making a mental note of which door he was behind, she vowed she would figure out a way to free him. Sera's toes were beginning to tingle as they reached the end of the white corridor, giving her hope that her muscle control would return soon. The President entered a code into the keypad beside a heavy metal door and swung it open. He flung Sera onto a chair in the middle of the cell and chained her to it. A feminine voice cried out. Sera wrenched her head up and located the owner.

A woman sat against the opposite wall, shackled in iron chains.

A woman with ginger hair.

Her mother.

Links

Get to know me by visiting:
altippett.com

Or by following my socials:
facebook.com/altippettauthor
instagram.com/a_l_tippett_author
tiktok.com/@altippettbooks
bookbub.com/profile/a-l-tippett
goodreads.com/altippett

Acknowledgements

Once again, I want to take a moment to thank you. Yes, you there, holding this book. Whether you are reading these pages on your Kindle, phone, tablet, or if you've got your hands wrapped around the spine of a paperback...I want to say a heartfelt thank you for reading this story.

I hope you loved reading it as much as I loved creating it. Now, I know I left things dangling off the highest cliff that ever hung, so make sure you leap straight into the final book in The MINATH Chronicles: *A Dragon's Soul*. And I do hope you get some sleep soon. #SorryNotSorry

If you enjoyed this book, please consider leaving a review on Amazon, BookBub, Goodreads, or my website. If you really loved it, feel free to shout it from the rooftops (or alternatively, in all your bookish groups on social media!) Authors rely on the passion of lovely readers like yourself to prove to others that our book is worth taking a chance on. I'm always happy for readers to reach out to me with constructive feedback; if you have any suggestions on improvements for future books please head to my website to get in touch.

I want to sincerely thank the professionals who helped make *A Dragon's Body* the best story that it could be. A special thanks to my editor, Sheryl Lee, whose advice and guidance is always appreciated. A massive thank you to my new designer, MiblArt, for the stunning cover.

I appreciate my wonderful beta readers, Kara and Claire, so much. Your feedback was extremely helpful and *A Dragon's Body* is a better story because of you. I am also very grateful to the wonderful members of 20Booksto50k® for sharing the details of their own journey up the mountain.

I can't even begin to thank all the family members and friends who have offered their support throughout my self-publishing journey. And to everyone who gave up their time to babysit my kids... you have my eternal gratitude; I wouldn't have finished this book without your help!

So many thanks and hugs for my parents for their unwavering support. Love you uttmasaba.

To my children, thank you for always making me laugh. And for your nose "boops" and for those sweet snuggles and even sweeter smiles. A little less grateful for the constant interruptions and the disrupted sleep, but hey, you win some, you lose some. I love you beyond words. You fill my heart with so much love and make everything worthwhile.

Fly fierce, strike strong.

April xo

About the Author

I was born in the South Island of New Zealand before my family and I moved to Australia when I was two years old. We lived on a yacht for a few years and travelled along the east coast of Aussie and across the Pacific Ocean to New Caledonia. My parents schooled us via Distance Education while we sailed the seas until we bought a house on the Sunshine Coast in Queensland. I finally got to go to "real-school" and loved it – I couldn't understand why we had weekends (because, apparently, I am, and always will be, a big nerd).

Shortly before beginning high school, we moved north to a rural property near Mackay. The big draw card was that I could finally buy my own horse, a dream I'd had since I was a little girl.

Then, I started writing. I began work on my first fantasy novel when I was twelve but abandoned it after deciding that being an author wasn't a "real" job and therefore not worth pursuing. After completing my secondary schooling, my parents encouraged me to experience the real world before committing to a university degree. So, I applied to be a rider in a travelling horse show! Unfortunately, I wasn't successful so instead I did the complete opposite and got a job as an insurance broker. I worked in insurance for seven years before leaving to start a family.

I am now the mother of two wonderful children. It's tricky finding the time to write with two young kids (whilst combatting sleep deprivation!) but, thankfully, I have a Will in my life now, and he helps me find a way. I can't wait to get started on my next book and am looking forward to sharing many more stories with you!